CARLOS RUBIO

Faded Dreams

A Cuban Memoir

First published by Editions Dedicaces in 2018

Copyright © Carlos Rubio, 2018

First edition

ISBN: 978-1-77076-728-7

This book was professionally typeset on Reedsy. Find out more at reedsy.com

To the memory of my parents,
who made my life possible
through their sacrifice.

To Carlos, Albert, and
Marisa, who provide me with
a sense of continuity.

And to Ethan and Liliana, for
they surely own the future.

Contents

Preface   iii
Other works by Carlos Rubio   iv
RECUERDOS/MEMORIES   1
CHOPIN   4
ABUELAS/GRANDMOTHERS   8
MARTÍ   13
PISTOLAS/GUNS   18
MECEDORAS/ROCKING CHAIRS   23
CUMPLEAÑOS/BIRTHDAY   26
TARARÁ   29
BAUTISMO/BAPTISM   34
GATO/CAT   39
SANTERÍA   42
CORRUPCIÓN/CORRUPTION   46
AMIGOS/FRIENDS   49
PUERTO ESPERANZA   53
SAN JUAN   63
COMUNIÓN/COMMUNION   68
FUNERAL   74
ANATOMÍA/ANATOMY   76
ALBINO   91
KARMA   96
BACHILLERATO/HIGH SCHOOL   101
PRESIDENTE/PRESIDENT   106

AVIONES/AIRPLANES 109
JAZZ 111
DESCONTROLADO/OUT OF CONTROL 114
VENGANZA/REVENGE 119
BARLOVENTO 123
SOLFEO/MUSIC THEORY 125
BOY SCOUTS 129
MOTOCICLETA/MOTORCYCLE 135
TOTA 140
MACHO/MALE 143
TESTOSTERONA/TESTOSTERONE 146
HUELGA/STRIKE 150
PASODOBLE 152
EUFORIA/EUPHORIA 155
PAREDÓN/FIRING SQUAD 157
VIOLACIÓN/VIOLATION 159
PRISIÓN/PRISON 162
TARZÁN/TARZAN 167
ARTISTA/ARTIST 172
NUNCA MÁS/NEVER MORE 176
SORPRESAS/SURPRISES 179
RESISTENCIA/RESISTANCE 184
ISIDRO 187
INVASIÓN/INVASION 192
ADIÓS/GOODBYE 195
REFLEXIONES/REFLECTIONS 201
Inside of my Cuban passport 203
My parents, Blanca and Luis Alberto 204
Luis in his Boy Scout Uniform 205
Vivian and Enrique, my closest friends 206
About the Author 207

Preface

I never intended to write this book. It was at the insistence of my children, but especially my daughter Marisa, that I reluctantly undertook this project. First of all, I do not believe that my early life in Cuba was that interesting, so this account would have no value except for the members of my family. Second, I am a novelist, and I am certain that the characters that I have created throughout my writing career are far more interesting than my life could ever be.

During the writing process, I had to revisit memories of events that took place long ago, and resurrect friends and family members who are no longer with us. They accompanied me every step of the way, like distant echoes from a past that reminded me of personal plans that were never realized—hence *Faded Dreams*. But secretly—I confess—I was flattered that my children should have shown an interest in the life of that boy who was born long ago in a distant land, whose life took an unexpected turn, and who ultimately became their father.

Other works by Carlos Rubio

Saga
Finalist Letras de Oro, 1993
Orpheus' Blues
Secret Memories/Recuerdos secretos
Quadrivium
Winner, Nuevo León International Prize for Novels, 1989
Dead Time/Tiempo muerto
Silver Medal, Book of the Year Awards, 2003
Orisha
Hubris
American Triptych
(*The Neophyte, Bullwhip, California Fever*)
Forgotten Objects
Finalist, Readers' Choice Awards, 2015

RECUERDOS/MEMORIES

I used to be immortal, but that was a long time ago when I believed that the course of my life was inalterable and that everything and everyone around me would go on forever. It was before I boarded a plane and vanished into thin air one afternoon in the summer of 1961. At that precise moment—although I did not realize it then—the man I was meant to become ceased to exist, and was inexorably transformed into someone whose future existence was as improbable as an ant fully understanding the designs of the Creator.

The Danish philosopher Soren Kierkegaard said that life could only be understood backwards, but that it had to be lived forward. He was right. Now with the perspective and clarity acquired over many years, I can see that what appeared at the time to be a series of random events was really a natural sequence that eventually created the man who writes these lines today.

But I get ahead of myself. That sense of immortality and invulnerability, I realize now, was nurtured in me by my entire family—but especially by my mother—for as far back as I can remember. The feeling that I had the right to be in this world, that anything was possible, was always present and it would prove invaluable many years later while making my way in a new and distant land with a new language and strange customs.

No one emerges from a void, but from a confluence of two

different families that fate chooses for you. That simple and random act of being born will determine what language you speak, what opportunities will be available to you, and generally how far you will get in life.

I was lucky. My mother, Blanca, a professor at the Normal School, and my father, Luis Alberto, a criminal lawyer, provided a stable and stimulating environment for me and for my younger brother, Luis. All this was reinforced by our aunts and uncles on both sides of the family.

Given the type and variety of visitors that we had on a regular basis, our household had to be one of the most interesting in the city of Pinar del Río, capital of the province bearing the same name and located west of Havana. My mother's friends were mostly teachers, writers, musicians and artists. Being as young as I was at the time, I was always in awe of the poets who showed up to do a reading of their latest work, the painters who frequently exhibited their canvases on our walls, or the guitarists who showed up after hours and played on well past midnight. Since my room was close to the library where these sessions usually took place, I would sneak out of bed and spy from the darkness—a perfect accomplice—on whatever was going on at the time.

My cousin Pablo, an accomplished painter and guitarist, showed up one particular night, carrying his guitar. The most vivid recollection I have of that event is not the music that he played, but how he had placed a lit cigarette between the strings and the neck of the guitar. As he ran his fingers up and down, pressing skillfully on the frets to invoke the appropriate chords, the ashes at the tip of the cigarette grew longer and longer. *They have to fall at any moment,* I kept telling myself, but they stubbornly clung to their original cylindrical form. At the conclusion of the piece, and realizing that the glowing tip was about to reach the wood of the neck, Puri—that was Pablo's nickname—removed the cigarette from its improvised holder and shook the ashes into a nearby ashtray.

The people who came to see my father were quite different. Even though he had his law practice in a separate building, he also kept an office in the back of our house. That meant, of course, that his clients had to traverse its entire length to see him. Those visitors were very unlike the intellectuals and artists who came to visit my mother. Just by looking at them one could tell they had other concerns—mostly legal—and besides looking preoccupied, some also appeared a little sinister. But once again I am getting ahead of myself, since I am speaking of a house that my parents did not acquire until 1950.

CHOPIN

O ur first house was not really ours, but a rental located on the corner of Cuartel and Yagruma. We lived on the ground floor and a young couple lived upstairs. I remember that he worked for Taca, a Cuban company that manufactured tee shirts, and that he sometimes gave us free samples that he brought home from the factory. He was tall, thin, and had dark hair. If I ever knew his name I have long since forgotten it, but I remember that we called him Papo.

That house, as small as it was, still had a backyard of sorts, with a clothes line that my brother Luis and I used for swinging and a small fountain usually full of tadpoles that we tried to catch, but always failed because either they were too quick or our hands were too small.

As with most Cuban or Latin American houses, this one also had an open front porch—*el portal*—equipped with the obligatory rocking chairs. In the evenings, after the sun went down and the air became cooler, one could sit there, read the paper or just watch whatever was going on in the street. It was not unusual for people to stop and engage in conversation with my parents for a while. At that time I just took everything for granted; I had no idea then that they came from two of the most prominent families in the city. To me they were just *Mami* and *Papi*.

That porch, by the way, was not at street level, but above it.

From the sidewalk one had to walk up about ten steps to reach the front door. This, I thought, was great because it afforded an unobstructed view of the intersection below.

One of my most vivid recollections is of the time they were repaving the street. Early one morning the crew just appeared, bearing an assortment of tools that I had never seen before. It did not take them long to start spreading the hot asphalt that cascaded down from the bed of a truck with a loud exhaust. But what caught my attention immediately was the massive steamroller—*la aplanadora*—that followed the truck. Standing on a small platform, like an immutable and impassive god, was a huge man with a cigar between his teeth and his belly protruding from his open shirt. As he pushed the different levers of the machine, he spewed the noxious fumes of the cigar into the morning air. From his improvised throne he seemed to rule the entire street. Even though the speed of the steamroller was minimal, everyone knew that they had to spread the asphalt that descended from the truck as quickly as possible and stay out of the way. *Of course! That is the job I want to have when I grow up.* What appealed to me was the sheer massiveness of the machine, the smoothness and solidity of its metal wheels, and its unstoppable and inexorable trajectory that forced everyone to stay ahead of it. As you may surmise, that wish never came to fruition; I have never even been on a steamroller, let alone operated one. By the end of the day, the workmen and the equipment were gone. All that was left was a brand-new street, the pungent smell of fresh asphalt and the indelible memory of that sweaty titan smoking a cigar and expertly riding the mechanical beast.

That *portal*, as I said before, gave us an advantageous position to observe the world outside our house. Sometimes, especially during the summer, there would be violent downpours often accompanied by thunder and lightning. I did not mind the rain but I was terrified of the thunder. My father, aware of this fact, was always prepared. Hidden in the side pockets of his jacket—he always wore a suit and a bow tie—he had an ample supply of Hershey's chocolate kisses. Whenever thunder broke out, he would toss a handful of candy on the floor, thus making me believe that the loud sound released the chocolates from above. As time passed, my fear waned and the thunderstorms did not bother me anymore.

Located diagonally from our house on Cuartel Street was the best bicycle shop in the city. Although I don't know how or why, Abigail, the owner, was a friend of the family. He was a short, stocky man with a kind disposition. I remember going into the showroom of the shop and wandering among the neat rows of shiny new bikes and looking at the array of accessories available. Abigail would always take the time to explain the difference between the bikes and how the accessories worked. Located below the showroom was the shop where bicycles were repaired. One of the mechanics was Rodolfo, a tall, black man who smiled often. He, too, was a friend of the family, so our visits to the shop were quite common. To this day, I have yet to figure out how Rodolfo became friends with our family.

Around that time, Teresa García—Luis and I called her Teté—a young woman who was barely out of her teens, came to work for the family. She had a number of sundry duties, but her main responsibility was looking after us. She made sure that we had clean clothes, were ready for our meals, and kept up with the many needs that very young children have. She stayed with us until both my father and mother died, and throughout the years she secured a place of trust within our family.

About four blocks away, going east on Yagruma, was the kindergarten where our formal education began. Señorita Lucrecia, the teacher, at one time or another must have had every person in town as a student, for when I first met her she was already very old. I remember some of the activities of those early days and the games we played during recess, but those memories are quite faint compared to the ones I have of señorita Lucrecia's assistant. She was a thin, young woman with raven-black hair and beautiful features. I know that I should remember her name, but memory is a tricky thing and that fact faded away long ago. What remained, after all these years, is the fragrance that she exuded when she came to visit, which was about twice a week.

During those visits, señorita Lucrecia would have the class sit around the piano that was located at the back of the room. This beautiful woman then played a type of music that I had never heard before—it was completely different from the tunes that were in vogue and that were constantly repeated on the radio. The music was somewhat melancholic, and I would always lose myself in its cadences. Of course, I was in love with that beautiful woman who could play such music and evoke in me feelings that I could not identify. Many years later, I realized that what she played were mazurkas by Chopin. Even to this day, Chopin has remained my favorite classical composer. Occasionally, I look at a photograph of my fifth birthday which was celebrated at the school. My mother baked a cake, all my classmates were there, and so were señorita Lucrecia and her assistant. Yet, I do not recall that day. As I said, memory is a very unreliable and selective thing.

ABUELAS/GRANDMOTHERS

The summer of 1950 was a particularly sad one. Rosa, my paternal grandmother, died. All my memories of her are fond ones, albeit rather spotty. By the time I met her she was in her eighties and could no longer walk.

Every afternoon, after taking a bath and putting on clean clothes, Luis and I would visit her. Sometimes we rode our tricycles and Teresa walked behind us on the sidewalk. Her house was on Martí Street, adjacent to my father's office, and since there was a connecting door between the two structures, he visited her several times a day.

Abuela Rosa—or Mamaíta, as we called her—always sat in the dining room next to a small open courtyard with lots of ferns and other tropical plants. She would rock slowly and talk to us about many things, but I think that she mostly wanted to listen to us because children bring with them a fresh and unspoiled perspective of the world, a certain magic that makes adults feel young again when they are in their presence.

From time to time, Mamaíta would light up a cigarette that she took out of a chainmail purse and exhaled the smoke softly. Whenever she did that, she also took several matches out of their box and tossed them onto the tiles that lined the courtyard. Luis and I would then step on the matches while simultaneously sliding our feet to make them light up. We thought it was fun and she loved the excitement that showed on our faces as we managed to light the matches that she had scattered on the floor.

A few days before her death, I was taken to see her. Of course, I had no idea what was going on, or that I would be saying goodbye for the last time. This time she was not in the usual rocking chair by the courtyard, but in her bedroom. As I was led into the room, I noticed immediately the clear oxygen tent over the bed; I had no idea what it was, nor did it occur to me to ask. Someone—I don't know who—opened the side of the tent so I could lean in and kiss Mamaíta. What sticks in my mind about that moment is not the waxen color of her face or her feeble respiration, but the noticeable drop in temperature inside the enclosure. The visit did not last long. I was whisked away and never saw her again.

I also remember Mamaíta as a very young woman (she could not have been more than eighteen) from a photograph taken around 1880 in an interior courtyard. Her parents are sitting in the foreground and their eight children are standing behind them. She was a very beautiful woman, with dark hair and classical features. I am sure that it was this beauty that captivated Buenaventura Carmelo Rubio, my grandfather.

Their story is a classic one of forbidden love, for he was also her half uncle. He came to Pinar del Río to visit his brother, and once uncle and niece met the attraction was immediate. The family, of course, was understandably concerned. Because of the close family ties, such a union would not be sanctioned by the church. But Rosa and Buenaventura would not be so easily deterred, even if it took them years. They filed a formal petition with the ROTA, that branch of the Vatican that rules on special dispensations. Eventually, they were granted permission and were married around 1884. They had five children, among them Luis Alberto, my father, who was born in August of 1887. All those children, of course, had Rubio Rubio as both their surnames. They all went on to pursue successful careers; Carmelo became a civil engineer, Carmen Rosa and María Rita became teachers, and Luis Alberto and Carlos became lawyers.

Many years later, while looking at old pictures of the family, it occurred to me that most of my ancestors did not have Cuban, but Spanish citizenship. At the time of their birth Cuba did not exist as an independent republic, but only as a colony. It was not until May 20th, 1902, after four years of American occupation, that the Cuban flag was raised for the first time. I have no idea how the transition was made from one citizenship to another or if there was a formal transition at all.

Abuela Paula, my maternal grandmother was quite different from Rosa. Unlike Rosa, who came from a wealthy family, she had more humble beginnings. She married Cristóbal Albet, my grandfather, and had eight children, among them Blanca, my mother. I am sure they struggled financially since his job working for *Obras Públicas*, the Cuban equivalent of the State Road Department, did not pay much. He also had a small farm and went out there every morning before dawn to milk the cows before going to his regular job.

Just as with Rosa, by the time I came along she was already old, maybe beyond her years due to frequent childbearing, constant work, and those unexpected reverses that life hands out to everyone. My mother once showed me a picture of her as a young woman and I was truly amazed. She had to be one the most beautiful women I have ever seen. No wonder my grandfather Cristóbal was so taken with her, but I will always remember her as old.

We did not see Poa—that's what we called her—on a regular basis since she did not stay in one place all the time. Sometimes she would stay with Tía Nena—the oldest of her children—in Havana for a few months, then come back to Pinar del Río. She did not live in town, but had a small farm called *Paso Viejo* located about six kilometers from the city. When she was there, we would try to visit often but it was not as simple as visiting Abuela Rosa, who lived just two blocks away. After leaving the main highway, the road that led to the farm was unpaved and its surface full of deep potholes that were often filled with water after the frequent rains. Driving a car on that road was a risky proposition, so we would hire people who had a jeep to take us out there.

Along that road there were no other houses, just a lot of trees—ceiba, mango and guava—that provided shade and fresh fruit all year long. Poa's house in *Paso Viejo* was not large but it was comfortable. There was a small flower garden in front of the porch where the traditional rocking chairs welcomed the occasional visitors. In the living room next to the wooden couch, there was a battery operated radio—there was no electricity in *Paso Viejo*—and a kerosene lamp stand mounted high on the wall. Beyond this point were the dining room, the two bedrooms, the kitchen, and the bathroom. In the kitchen pantry, always within easy reach, Poa kept a bottle of *Anís del Mono*, an anisette drink imported from Spain. Whenever she took a drink, of course, it was for 'medicinal' purposes. All the rooms were small, but the house was more than adequate for just one person. Behind the house, facing a sugarcane field, was a concrete patio.

From time to time, family reunions would take place in *Paso Viejo*. During these occasions Poa's eight children would come from Pinar del Río or Havana and renew their relationship with their mother and each other. Next to Poa's house there was an open wall pavilion surrounded by eucalyptus trees whose roof was made of the thatch of royal palms that are so abundant in Cuba. Several tables would be set up and during the early afternoon the meal would be served. It usually consisted of roasted pig prepared in an open pit, rice, black beans, and yucca, perhaps the favorite root of most Cubans. There would also be a variety of desserts and an assortment of wines. The preparation of such a feast took hours and all the women shared equally in this endeavor. It was a ritual that took place at least once a year and that everyone made an effort not to miss.

Cuban children have always enjoyed a privileged position within families, so everyone went out of their way to spend time with us. Besides, there were only three children at that time: Luis and me, and our cousin Bertica from Havana. My other aunts were still single, so they had not had any children yet. *Paso Viejo* was always fun and Luis and I even celebrated some early birthdays there.

The only person missing from these family reunions was my grandfather Cristóbal; by then he had already died, so I do not have any recollections of him.

MARTÍ

D uring the fall of 1950 I entered first grade. The school was located at the top of the hill on Cuartel Street. Unlike kindergarten, I had to wear a uniform: dark blue knickers, white shirt, and blue tie. Every day I made my way up the hill, carrying a briefcase with my school supplies, and spent the morning in a class of about thirty students. Gone were the simple activities that señorita Lucrecia would have us do in kindergarten and the games I played with my classmates. Now we had to sit in class all morning, pay attention to the teacher, and do less than interesting tasks. I longed for the melancholic sound of Chopin's mazurkas and the ineffable fragrance of señorita Lucrecia's assistant.

My favorite part of the morning was recess. They used to sell *acemitas*—sweet buns—for one centavo, and I bought one every day and ate it while sitting at the base of a marble obelisk that was located at the center of the ample courtyard. I could have bought more than one, since my mother gave me five centavos every day before leaving the house, but I saved my money and put the remaining four centavos in a bank shaped like a boot as soon as I came home.

I found out many years later that the school had been built on the site of a former army barracks or garrison, which is precisely what the word Cuartel means in Spanish, and that one of the most horrific events in the history of the city had taken place there. The year was 1910, and they were loading boxes of explosives onto carts in order to transport them. There was a loose board on the lid of one of the boxes and the man in charge ordered a carpenter to nail it shut. As soon as the hammer hit the nail, a massive explosion was set off. The entire barracks was demolished and the northern section of the city was covered in a rain of stone and debris—some people in the city believed that it had to do with Halley's Comet—and there were many dead and injured. That marble obelisk, at whose base a first grader would sit many years later obliviously eating sweet bread, commemorated that event and the lives that were lost that fateful day.

During the middle of the school year, my parents told me that we would be leaving the house at Cuartel and Yagruma. Apparently, my father had won a very important case and part of his fee was a house located on Martí Street, across from Independence Park. This was one of the most desirable—and expensive—locations in the city. Besides being located on the main street of the town, it was relatively close to my father's office. Even though he always owned a car, he preferred to walk.

I must confess that I was not impressed, given its state of disrepair, when I saw the new house. The main advantage, from my point of view, was its location. Every year, the streets leading to Independence Park were blocked off and a fair, or *tómbola*, was held. A small admission fee had to be paid to attend, but since the new house was already inside the confines of the fair, we could attend free of charge.

This fair went on for several evenings, and they had something for everybody. Children enjoyed a wishing well, cotton candy, and other treats. For the adults there was a shooting gallery and games of chance where all sorts of prizes could be won. My favorite game—strictly limited to adults—was the Treasure Bucket. It was a simple game, really, but one that was not easily mastered. At the bottom of a galvanized metal bucket filled with water, around twenty or thirty one peso coins had been placed. These coins were exactly the size of an American dollar and also made of silver. For the price of a nickel, those willing to try could dip their hands in the bucket and grab as many coins as they could. It looked easy enough, except for one catch: the bucket had been electrified. Many tried, but I do not recall anyone succeeding. I have no idea how many volts were running though the water, but as soon as the hand broke its surface, the men would instinctively jump back, repelled by the electric charge. Most tried to do it quickly, but even if they succeeded in withstanding the tremendous discomfort, the electricity caused their muscles to tighten, thereby making them lose control of their hand. These repeated failures, one would think, would deter others from trying but the line for the Treasure Bucket formed early and was always a long one.

Beside these yearly *tómbolas,* another advantage of living right across from Independence Park was the weekly *retretas,* or public concerts. Myriad folding chairs were arranged in concentric circles around the huge *glorieta,* or gazebo, where the musicians from the municipal band would converge later that day once the sun set and the temperature became more tolerable.

I liked the fact that their uniforms were always heavily starched and perfectly pressed and that they arranged their music stands in a symmetrical pattern. These, of course, were some minor details. Most important was the music itself—mostly *danzones,* a type of nostalgic composition that became part of Cuban musical tradition in the 19th century, but whose popularity has not

15

waned, even to the present day.

By the time they started to play the first piece of the evening, the park was filled to capacity. Those latecomers who had not managed to find a seat would linger on the fringes of the music, where the vendors had set up their makeshift stands and dispensed fruit juices, candy, and other treats.

My parents usually sat in the rocking chairs that we had on the *portal* while Luis and I roamed around the park with other boys and just enjoyed the music and the mercurial and amorphous crowd that never failed to materialize for those musical evenings. Yes, living right across from Independence Park had some definite advantages.

Although the new house was much larger than the one on Cuartel and Yagruma, it needed lots of work, but my mother was well aware of that fact. Besides that house, part of my father's legal fee was in cash, so that money was used to bring the house up to par. Two new bathrooms were added and the floor of the first courtyard was redone with red tile with three green squares accenting the middle. The dining room was also redone to my mother's specifications. After all the work was completed, the entire house was painted. The first bedroom (the one closest to the street) was occupied by my parents, Luis and I had the second one, and our cousin Candelaria, whom we called Tata, had the fourth one. The third one was kept as a guest room, and my mother decorated it in a Chinese motif. The furniture was red and black lacquered wood with carved bas-relief water lilies. It was a beautiful room, but what I liked best about it was a porcelain statue of a Chinaman. His hands could be removed and stored in a small box. I assume you would ask that deity for a favor, remove his hands, and not replace them until the wish was granted. This particular image served me well, for I used it as a central theme many years later in one of my novels entitled *Secret Memories*.

The house also had a second courtyard with a central orange tree and flowerbeds along the brick and a stucco wall that surrounded it. Off the second courtyard there was a fifth bedroom with a full bath but it was seldom, if ever, used.

At last, after many months of constant renovations, upgrades, and a final coat of fresh paint, the house was transformed from a musty, almost somber building into one full of light and with all the modern conveniences. I would live in that house for exactly eleven years until my departure to the United States.

Although my brother Luis and I could not do much to help with the move, there were some things that we transported in Luis' red wagon. More specifically, I remember when we took a plaster bust of Isidro from the house on Cuartel to the one on Martí.

According to my mother, many years before, Isidro had been a boy of flesh and blood. Because of his bad behavior and his constant disobedience, as punishment he had been transformed into a lifeless bust. Not until he found a house whose children showed exemplary behavior, retained their innocence, and always obeyed their parents would he be transformed into a boy once again. In our new house he enjoyed a place of prominence in the living room, resting on a carved pedestal and surveying with his blind eyes all who entered or left the house.

Isidro's tale was one often invoked by my mother when Luis and I were beginning to misbehave. She reminded us that we did not want to make Isidro wait one more day until such a time when he was returned to life. We reacted favorably to her admonitions and immediately stopped whatever mischief we were doing.

PISTOLAS/GUNS

B eyond the main living room—*la sala*—was a smaller room—*la saleta*—where my father had his easy chair and an old tube radio where he listened to opera or the news as he rested in the evenings. Separating these two rooms was a dividing wall that rose about four feet and had shelves on both sides. On the living room side, my mother displayed some porcelain and other decorations. On the *saleta* side, however, the shelves were replete with trophies that my father had won as a sharp shooter with his .38 caliber revolver. The centerpiece of the trophies was a huge cup, I estimate about two feet tall, made of silver. The engraving on its surface proclaimed Dr. Luis Alberto Rubio as the best shooter in Cuba in the year of 1933.

At the time, of course, being as young as I was, I did not really pay much attention to all the trophies or their meaning. After all, everything had happened before my birth, so it was all very distant and removed. As I got older, though, I became more interested in the history behind those pieces and what I found out was both truly fascinating and amazing at the same time.

For many years my father had been practicing with his .38 and often entered shooting tournaments throughout the island. He bought his ammunition directly from the United States; in the backyard of his law office the walls had been lined with steel plates, just to make sure that no bullets would go beyond those confines.

Every day he would shoot one hundred rounds, fifty in the morning and fifty in the afternoon, and his skill as a marksman was legendary in our province. His confidence with the revolver was so great that every day, during the afternoon practice sessions, he staged a display of his undisputed mastery (I want to add that to this day I consider this exhibition inexcusable and reckless behavior).

A man named Antonio, but whom everyone called Ñico, would stand in front of the wall, where the targets were located, with a piece of fruit on his head. Everyone fell silent. Then my father, with absolute concentration, would aim and shoot the fruit off Ñico's head. This was a show that went on for a long time and always drew a lot of people.

I often wonder how long this would have continued had the hand of fate not intervened. And maybe what happened next was just as well, for a needless tragedy was probably averted: my father gradually lost his eyesight, until he became completely blind. There was no logical explanation; there had been no trauma or injuries. It just happened. This loss of sight was accompanied by pain, which could only be alleviated by heat. In the evenings, to help him sleep, Ñico would set some papers on fire inside a metal trashcan to raise the temperature near his bed.

Since the doctors in Pinar del Río were baffled by his condition, several specialists were consulted in Havana. One of these doctors suggested that if all his teeth were extracted, his eyesight might return. This, of course, was a dreadful alternative, since my father had a perfectly good set of teeth. I suspect that the prospect of being blind the rest of his life—hence no better than an invalid—prompted him to make that decision. I can only imagine the pain of such procedure, but that was not the worst of it. His eyesight did not return.

There were no alternatives left, at least not in Cuba. So, he decided to travel to New York in order to consult Dr. Castroviejo, a Spanish surgeon who pioneered cornea transplants and one of the foremost ophthalmologists in the world at that time.

After the initial consultation and a series of examinations, Dr. Castroviejo told my father that there was nothing wrong with his eyes; his problem was one that had originated in a diet full of fatty foods. His optic nerves had been coated with a layer of cholesterol, thus impeding his vision. He was then referred to another specialist, who prescribed a very strict low-fat diet and a regimen of daily exercise. After a while, his vision gradually returned to normal. After that episode, he no longer ate any red meat or anything fried. He limited himself to fruit, vegetables, and a small piece of roasted chicken breast in the evenings for the rest of his life.

Of course, I have no memory of these events, since they took place years before I was born. I do remember, however, the steel plates that lined the walls in the backyard of my father's office. I would run my fingers on their surface and try to imagine all the people gathered there in the afternoons as he shot an apple, pear, or orange off Ñico's head.

Years later, while attending high school, I had the opportunity to speak to Ñico about those events. I could not conceive (and I still can't) why anyone would risk his life unnecessarily.

"Why would you do such a thing?" I asked him.

"I have always trusted your father completely," he answered me without hesitation.

"It is not a matter of trust," I retorted, "I would not even put a watermelon on my head for anybody. A bullet could have been defective from the factory," I reasoned, "and it would have hit you right on the forehead."

"But I am still here," he simply said and smiled. Perhaps he believed that every man has an appointed time with death and his had not come yet. Ñico died years later of liver cancer. I went to see him at the hospital during his final days and I am certain that he appreciated my visit, since he knew it would probably be the last one.

Another remnant of those years, more palpable and present in our house, was my father's gun collection. On the wall behind his desk there were eight or ten pistols and revolvers mounted on the wall. Later I would learn that those weapons were used as evidence in criminal cases that he had handled, and that each had killed at least one man.

In an unlocked closet next to the dining room, there was a veritable arsenal available for inspection, but they were mostly antique pieces: a Derringer, a .22 with four barrels and other sundry weapons. My two favorite pieces, however, were a cane whose handle—with a built-in firing pin—could be unscrewed and a shotgun cartridge placed inside the body, thus transforming it into a deadly weapon. The other one was a .38 revolver issued to the French police; its drum held seven bullets instead of the usual six. It was nice to keep a little surprise in reserve, I thought, just in case. There was also a .45 caliber pistol, but I always felt that it was too heavy to handle. I should add that although all those guns were readily accessible to us, my father had made sure that not a single bullet could be found in the entire house. I suppose that was a different era, in which it was not unusual for men to carry weapons as naturally as they carried change in their pockets.

Although I have never owned a gun as an adult, all this knowledge, acquired so early in my life, would later surface in the opening chapter of my novel *Dead Time*. As the main character cleans his weapon, in anticipation of killing a man later that day, all the parts of a gun are described and enumerated.

MECEDORAS/ROCKING CHAIRS

There was one particular incident at the time of the move to the new house that made me realize, although I did not know exactly how, that my father had a certain amount of influence in the town and some direct connections to the underworld. It is common for Cuban homes to have rocking chairs on the front porch; people sit, read the paper, or just watch the passersby, occasionally striking up conversations with friends or casual acquaintances. The family, along with the rest of our possessions, had transported the rocking chairs from our house on Cuartel to the new one on Martí. These rocking chairs were never brought into the house, but were always left out on the porch.

One morning, they were gone. My father did not seem to be very upset. I realize now that he had ways, due to his constant dealings with people who broke the law, of finding out who had taken them. He simply put out the word that he wanted his rocking chairs back.

A few days later, a man showed up at his office. His nickname was Cangrejo—Spanish for crab—a petty thief who operated in our town. Apparently, he was in my father's debt, for his tone was apologetic.

"I am sorry about the rocking chairs, Doctor," he said, "I just did not realize that you had moved to a new house; you will have them back right away."

My father never had any intentions of pressing charges, so he told Cangrejo that there was no harm done.

"Just one more thing," said Cangrejo before leaving the office, "I already had the rocking chairs painted; do you think you could reimburse me for the price of the paint?"

My father must have found this request amusing, for he did give the man some money for the paint and his trouble. The rocking chairs were back on our porch before the end of the day.

As I became older and more aware of what was going on around me, time and time again I would see evidence of how far-reaching his influence was, not just in our town but in the entire province as well.

The move from the house on Cuartel to the one on Martí, as I said before, took place during the middle of the school year. I still attended school at the same place, but now had to walk a few extra blocks. This did not bother me at all, until one day after dismissal.

As I walked downhill on Cuartel, I realized that I had to go to the bathroom. At that point I was exactly half way home, and by the time I got to the bottom of the hill, across from the bicycle shop, I was no longer walking, but running. After passing our former house on the corner, I realized that I would never make it home, so I went into the garage of a partially built house. I dropped my briefcase on the cement floor and desperately fumbled with the buttons of my pants, trying to open my fly. But it was too late. I felt a warm and steady stream coming down my leg, collecting momentarily at the bottom of my knickers and then slithering down into my shoe. There was nothing I could do; I ran home, crying. My mother must have thought there was something seriously wrong with me, but when she realized what had happened she simply laughed and took me into the bathroom so I could clean up and put on a fresh set of clothes, all the while reassuring me everything was alright and that sometimes accidents just happen.

CUMPLEAÑOS/BIRTHDAY

T hat spring, my parents decided to have a lavish party to celebrate my seventh birthday. I suspect that they also wanted to show off their newly refurbished house across from Independence Park. Formal invitations were printed and sent out to the families who had children of my approximate age. This was to be a costume party, with a special performance by Alexander, the magician.

Fully aware that I listened to The Adventures of Prince Tamakún every day, my mother decided that there could not be a more appropriate costume for me. Of course, such a costume was not available at any store, so it had to be homemade. Since Prince Tamakún was a radio show, no one had actually seen his garb. This fact did not deter my mother in the least. Given her many talents—after all, she was the founder of the *Escuela del Hogar*, or Home Economics School, in our town—she and my aunt Panchita went to work on the costume. It consisted of white satin pants and shirt of the same material but reddish in color. There was an accompanying sash decorated with sequins and another ornament—made of black beads—covering the right arm. Crowning the elaborate ensemble was a beautiful turban, also decorated with sequins and a feather. But this was not all; even the shoes had been transformed into golden footwear whose look was enhanced by matching buckles. It was perfect. It was, indeed, the costume of Prince Tamakún.

For my brother Luis she created a costume that was just as elaborate but that did not require as much imagination. He would appear at the party disguised as a bullfighter. Just to sew all the sequins on his cape and make the special hat must have taken an eternity, but my mother and Tía Panchita were meticulous and patient women who wanted everything to be perfect for that special day.

And perfect it was. Over one hundred children came to the party, including Tutico and Berta, my cousins from Havana. I am sure that I received many presents on that day, but I can't recall any of them in particular. The early part of the afternoon was spent playing games—such as pinning the tail on the donkey—that my parents had set up in the ample courtyard. Once all the games had been exhausted and the corresponding prizes awarded, the entire group moved into the dining room. We gathered around the traditional birthday cake that my mother had placed on the central table and sang happy birthday. Now it was time to move back to the courtyard where a huge and colorful piñata, in the shape of a merry-go-round, had been set up earlier. Cuban piñatas, unlike those popular in Mexico, were never beaten with a stick until they broke. They were constructed in such a way that myriad strings hung from their bottom—in this case the flat underside of the bright merry-go-around. After everyone had finished their piece of cake, we gathered under the piñata and held a string. Someone in the house, I can't remember who, counted to three and we all pulled on the strings simultaneously. As the bottom of the piñata collapsed, at once there was a deluge of candy, gum, and small prizes. We scrambled on the floor, our eager hands trying to capture as much booty as we could and stuff in our pockets.

The pièce de résistance came at the end of the afternoon. As mentioned earlier, Alexander the magician was to perform at the party. Magically, he was standing at one end of the courtyard—most likely he came in while we were busy harvesting the treasures from the piñata—ready to start the performance. He was tall, had black hair, and wore a suit. At once we all sat in folding chairs that had been rented for the occasion and were silent.

He performed one magic trick after another, each more amazing that the previous one. We all were, literally, under his spell. At one point during the performance I was summoned to join him; of course, I had no idea what he had in mind or what I was supposed to do. Alexander did not give me any instructions, but simply reached over to my right ear (the same ear that miraculously was not permanently damaged while attending second grade, but more about that later) and by just touching it, magically produced a veritable cascade of silver coins that he caught in a bowl he was holding with the other hand.

At the conclusion of Alexander's performance, the guests started to leave. It had been a most memorable day, one that I would always remember because of my friends, the games, the special costumes, and everything else that comes along with a special party. I never stopped to consider how much effort and money it must have taken to stage such a special event. I already said how lucky I was that fate had given me such great parents.

TARARÁ

A few months later, during the summer of 1951, one of my father's clients lent us a house at Tarará Beach, just a few miles from Havana. I remember it as a large, airy house where aunts and uncles from my mother's side of the family visited often. That summer was unforgettable, not because anything momentous happened, but because for the first time I had an absolute freedom to do anything I wanted. I soon made friends with other boys and we rode our bicycles everywhere without any adult supervision.

In the evenings, in order to control the mosquito population, a fumigating jeep would slowly traverse the streets, spewing thick columns of poisonous clouds from a rear device and bringing the visibility down to nothing. As soon the jeep appeared, as if it were the pied piper; all the kids from every house followed it, screaming with joy as we lost ourselves in the thick and noxious volutes. No one's parents seemed to be concerned about the number of brains cells we were losing by the minute as we inhaled the insecticides, a lethal cocktail of DDT and who knows what else. After all, we were just kids who were playing a harmless game. This day and age, no doubt, the EPA inspectors would put a stop to such reckless and irresponsible behavior very quickly.

On one occasion, my uncle Cristóbal came to visit. With him were his wife Berta and his daughter Bertica. One of eight children, from an early age he had shown a keen intelligence and the belief that the only way to get ahead in life was through education. He kept top grades in his studies and worked the ticket counter at the Milanés Theater—the first in the city of Pinar del Río. Eventually he went to medical school in Havana with a series of scholarships from the Masons. Now he had a medical practice in Marianao, a section of Havana. He was perhaps the most colorful uncle in the family and we always looked forward to his visits. In fact, my mother, rather that telling us bedtime stories, would substitute them with stories about her brother and all the pranks that he pulled off as a child. They were certainly a lot more interesting than fairy tales about princesses and mythical kingdoms, although sometimes they did not have happy endings but one that often included getting a belt whipping from Abuelo Cristóbal.

During that particular visit, I remember that my cousin Bertica (who would later become a physician herself) had a remote-controlled car, something that I had never seen before. But that was not the biggest surprise. From the trunk of his car, Uncle Joya (a nickname he had earned early in life, since he was the 'Jewel' of the family) produced a bird cage made of thin reeds and wire. But this was not a typical cage just meant to hold a bird. On either side of the main section, it was fitted with spring-loaded traps. There was a section on the top where bait—rice or other grains—would be placed. If a bird, attracted by the food landed on this platform, the cocked springs would be released, the entire top would quickly flip, and the unsuspecting bird would find itself inside the cage. It was a simple and elegant mechanism. I don't know why Uncle Joya had such a device or why he had brought it with him during that visit. Before long he had set up the cage, using rice as bait, and placed it on the ground about twenty or thirty feet away from the house. We all sat on the open porch, our eyes fixed on the cage. Our wait was not a long one; a small bird soon landed on the trap, the mechanism worked flawlessly, and the cage was no longer empty. We were all excited, of course, but what surprised me most about that day was not the capture of the bird, but what Uncle Joya did next. He walked over to the cage, picked it up slowly (was he trying to be dramatic purposely?), and then proceeded to make a speech stating that even though sometimes everyone could be trapped by circumstances, every creature had the right to be free. As he said this, he opened the door of the cage, put his hand around the bird inside, brought it out, and then released it into the morning air. This was a lesson that stayed with me. Many years later, this episode would be the basis for one of my short stories called *On The Way Up*, about a man trapped by circumstances and how he eventually attained his freedom.

Besides riding bicycles during the day, running behind the fumigating Tifa jeep at night, and sharing time with visiting relatives, we went to the beach every morning. The breaking of the waves on the shore was anything but gentle, and if we were not careful, the force of the water would knock us down. Every wave that broke on that beach was a surprise. Most of the time, they brought with them shells that we collected, but one particular occasion I found a gold watch—minus the crystal—that I quickly grabbed before it disappeared again into the surf. Of course, the watch was not in working condition, but months later I sold it to a jewelry shop in Pinar del Río.

The only event that marred all the fun we had that summer was a most unexpected one. A friend of the family was getting married and she needed a ring bearer in order to complete her wedding party. Imagine my dismay when my parents informed me that I would be leaving the beach for a few days to attend the stuffy wedding rehearsals and eventually walk down the aisle in an uncomfortable suit, holding a cushion with the rings, while a girl I did not even know tossed flower petals in the path of the bride. I was not happy at all. To this day I can still feel the overly starched collar of the dress shirt mercilessly constricting all movements of my neck.

Our uncle Justo, (Joya's older brother), called me aside a few days before the wedding and offered me five pesos if during the ceremony I tossed the cushion with the rings up into the air and ran out of the church. I can't say that I really considered his offer, but I never forgot it. He had the reputation of being an eccentric, and it was probably well deserved.

Just like Uncle Joya, he had put himself through school. As a boy he would get up before dawn to help Cristóbal, our grandfather, milk the cows they owned and then he would get ready for school. My mother told me once that on one occasion he got entangled in a barbed wire fence and came home with his head drenched in blood. Life had to be hard; after all, he was the older brother in a family of six girls and two boys.

During his high school years, he held a job as a kitchen helper at the Hotel Ricardo, one of the oldest in Pinar del Río. That money was used to help with the family expenses. Eventually he entered the University of Havana where he received a doctorate degree in the Humanities. For a number of years he was a teacher, but he made his mark—and his money—by writing a series of textbooks for the different levels of elementary education. These textbooks were adopted by many school districts in Cuba and I still have one of them in my personal library. Toward the end of his life, he became almost a recluse. I will mention him again later, for he provided me with the most incredible experience I ever had in my entire life.

It was also during that summer in Tarará that Luis and I saw for the first time a television commercial for a chocolate drink. It was called Kresto and it showed a piglet (El Cochinito Campeón) running and then sliding towards the drink. So impressed were my brother and I with that commercial, that as soon as we returned to Pinar del Río we decided to reenact the commercial at home. Somehow, we had to find a way of running and sliding just like the Cochinito Campeón.

Less than a year before, during the renovation of the house, new tiles had been put down on the courtyard, so Luis and I very diligently plugged shut the central drain with newspapers and connected a hose to a corner faucet. As the water flowed, having nowhere to go, it completely covered the surface of the courtyard about an inch deep. The wet and slippery tile provided the right setting to stage what we had seen on TV. Needless to say, any type of clothing, like a bathing suit, would have created too much friction so we had to take everything off. We ran and then slid on the wet surface, all the while shouting, "El Cochinito Campeón!"

My parents did not object in any way to this activity; in fact, they found it most amusing and we played that game many times for years to come.

BAUTISMO/BAPTISM

At the end of that summer, our family returned to Havana for a special event. Our aunt Estrella had her first baby—a girl who was named after her—and we were going to attend the baptism. We always stayed at Tía Carmen's house in the old section of Havana; she was the oldest of the eight children and everyone called her Nena. She lived on Hospital Street on the fifth or sixth floor of a building that had been erected at the turn of the century. It had an austere façade and the steps on the stairs were marble. The doors on the different landings corresponded to each of the dwellings. But Tía Nena's place was a little different, for it had two doors instead of one. The main door, which led to the living room, was wide; the other one, much narrower, led into a side room.

For some unknown reason, I found this interesting. I also reasoned that logically each apartment or floor needed a *puerta*—a door—but not two. To differentiate them, I named the main one *portañuela*—Spanish for the fly on your pants—and the smaller one *mininuela,* a meaningless word that contained the prefix mini to denote its smaller size. Perhaps this was an early sign of my interest in languages.

Of all the sisters, Tía Nena was the most religious. I do not mean to imply that my mother and other aunts did not believe in God, they just did not attend church on a regular basis. During my visits to Havana, I would occasionally ask Tía Nena to take me to toy stores, including the local branch of Woolworth's. She would say yes, but during those outings we always visited a church for a short time. I can still smell the incense, see the short votive candles burning in their red cups, and remember the faint light reflected on the gilded decorations of the baroque altars. These were, I now realize, very private moments that somehow she wanted to share with me but unfortunately I was just thinking about the new toys that I could get during that visit.

At that time, Uncle Justo lived with her and occupied one of the rooms where he kept a roll-top desk and an assortment of books and other odd but interesting items. As I mentioned before, he always had the reputation for being somewhat eccentric.

Spending time at Tía Nena's house was always fun. Her living room furniture had some very intricate carvings, which were ideal for strategically placing my collection of miniature soldiers and staging imaginary battles between opposing armies. There was also a balcony from which one could watch the entire street below. This was a novelty, since our house in Pinar del Río only had one floor.

At the corner of San Lázaro and Hospital there was a *bodega*, or grocery store. Since the building lacked an elevator, the tenants had resorted to a clever method so they would not have to walk all the flights of stairs when they wanted something. They simply called ahead and from the balcony lowered the money in a basket attached to a rope. One of the clerks from the *bodega* would cross the street and place the items in the basket, which was then pulled back up to the balcony.

After I finished deploying the infantry on Tía Nena's coffee table, I always called the *bodega* and ordered an Orange Crush since that drink was difficult to find in Pinar del Río. It was fun placing the five cent coin in the basket, lowering it to street level, and then retrieving the prize.

On the day of Estrellita's baptism, the weather was sunny and mild. I cannot recall what the exact arrangements were but I ended up in the back seat of Uncle Justo's car. On that day he wore a sober suit, tie, and dark glasses. Sitting next to him was Tía Mercedes, another one of my mother's sisters. Unlike Tía Nena and Tía Estrella, she lived in Pinar del Río and not in Havana. Somehow she had made the trek to attend the ceremony. Of all my aunts, Tía Mercedes was unique in many ways. What I remember most about her were her very light blue eyes and her blonde eyelashes. But her uniqueness went beyond her physical traits; she always told me stories about the members of the family and about Acevedo, her late husband, whom I never had a chance to meet. They never had any children of their own, but adopted a girl named Dora who would later become a teacher and marry into the Rubio family.

Tía Mercedes was a devotee of Saint John Bosco and also held the firm belief that one could communicate with the dead. Once she told me that when her husband was dying, he described to her some of the beautiful gardens that were found in heaven. One could explain this vision by citing the massive amount of endorphins with which the brain is flooded during its final moments, but there was another story for which I still have not found a logical answer.

After Acevedo's death, she often communicated with him using a Ouija board. Once again, one could simply say that people believe what they want to believe, that Tía Mercedes just moved the planchette in the direction of the letters that she subconsciously wanted to see. What I cannot explain is that on several occasions, during Valentine's Day, she won money in the national lottery. Without my asking her, she simply told me that Acevedo had communicated the winning numbers through the Ouija board.

At the beginning of November, on All Saints Day, she would go to the cemetery to take flowers and just clean around the mausoleum of the Albet family, where my grandfather Cristóbal was buried, and also to visit Acevedo's grave. I visited the cemetery many times with her, and on the way she would tell me all sorts of stories.

After we went through the wrought iron gates, and on the way to the Albet mausoleum, there was a grave that I particularly liked. According to Tía Mercedes, a young boy was buried there. His death had been the cause of a very unfortunate accident while flying a kite. In order to catch a better wind, he had climbed to the flat roof of his house. As the kite rose, he kept tugging on the string and walking backwards as he maneuvered it. Since there was no railing, he eventually fell off the edge of the roof and died as a result of this fall.

In one of his pants pockets they found a handful of colorful marbles that he had been carrying around with him, perhaps for a game later that day. On his grave, and as remembrance, these marbles had been carefully embedded in the stone. Since we had to go by his grave to our family's pantheon, I always asked Tía Mercedes to stop there for a few minutes so I could look at the marbles again.

For the baptism in Havana, since it was a special occasion, Tía Mercedes had on a gray dress and also wore a hat; at that time it was not permissible for women to enter a Catholic church without some sort of covering on their heads.

As we left the center of the city and onto the highway that led to the church, the soft breeze came in through the open windows of the car. Uncle Justo and Tía Mercedes were talking about something that must not have been very important to me. What held my interest on that sunny morning was Tía Mercedes' hat. The focal point of that headpiece was a real bird, pointing forward, that had somehow been mounted on its surface; it appeared, at least to me, that at any moment it would fly away. But as we progressed on the way to the church, enveloped by the breeze that was amplified by the speed of the car, the bird remained on its unnatural perch. Yet, I knew that it wanted to fly; it needed to fly, to return to the air, its natural medium of which it had been deprived for so long.

Inexplicably, something came over me. A force that overpowered my will and compelled me to leap forward, grab the hat off Tía Mercedes' head and toss it out the window as far as I could. The bird had finally been freed!

My actions had been so swift and unexpected that neither my uncle nor my aunt had time to react. Uncle Justo, of course, stopped the car, placed it in reverse and a few hundred yards back found the hat, still intact, resting on the curb.

We went on to the church, but Tía Mercedes did not put her hat back on until we were about to go into the building. The baptism proceeded as planned, and afterwards there was a family celebration, but I remember nothing about it.

GATO/CAT

That fall I entered second grade, but since we had moved, I did not go back to the school at the top of the hill on Cuartel Street. Several blocks away, also on Martí Street, was my new school—la Escuela Anexa a la Normal—an elementary school that was somehow linked to the Normal School where my mother taught. The colors of the uniform were the same as those at Cuartel, but rather than wearing knickers we just wore regular pants. I liked that; after all, I did not want to be reminded of that unfortunate incident when I lost control of my bladder and the warm stream momentarily collected around the elastic band of the pant leg before proceeding into the recesses of my shoe.

The school building was set back from the street, separated from the traffic by a small park. There were concrete benches on the sidewalk and the entire length of the park was lined with almond trees that provided a welcome shade from the relentless Cuban sun. The school was also higher than street level, so in order to get to its front door, one would climb a set of stairs and reach a semicircular path—one could either go left or right—that led to the entrance.

At the Escuela Anexa there were two second grade sections. I don't know why I was assigned to Diana Cuervo's class; perhaps because the Rubios were linked to the Cuervos by marriage, but that is just pure speculation on my part.

Diana Cuervo had the reputation of being the meanest teacher at the school. As the school year progressed, I soon came to the conclusion that her reputation was well deserved. During our penmanship exercises she would walk around the room with a stern face and a short wooden rod in her hand. If a student was not shaping the letters to her satisfaction, or if he went outside the limiting lines printed on the page, she was quick to crack the knuckles of the infractor with the merciless rod.

Besides practicing penmanship, we also took dictation on a regular basis. She read the words while walking around the room and checking for spelling. During one of those sessions, the word on the list was *Gato*, which is the Spanish word for cat. Not a very difficult word, but that morning I was unfortunate enough to misspell it. By substituting the initial G with a J, I had gone from *Gato* to *Jato*; from Cat to a meaningless concept. Upon seeing this error, Diana Cuervo was incensed. Bending down quickly, she pulled my ear, brought her mouth very close and shouted into it the correct syllable, "GAAAAAA!!!" Needless to say, I never made that mistake again.

If I were to say that she picked on me I would be lying, for she chastised every student with equal swiftness and severity. Everyone except for Gustavito Cuervo, who just happened to be her nephew. Not wanting to show the slightest favoritism, she expected him to exceed the expectations she had for the class, not just academically, but in accuracy and promptness with his work. He often failed.

Gustavito lived across the street from the school, so there was really no excuse for being tardy. I don't know whether he liked to stay in bed or took too long eating breakfast, but he was often a few minutes late. This flagrant disregard for punctuality and decorum could not be tolerated. Diana Cuervo stood by the door, waiting. As soon as he arrived, he was greeted with a violent slap on the back of the head. Then he would be led across the room and shoved forcefully into his desk. What a way to start the day.

While the children in the class were corrected with the intimidating rod and an occasional shout, Gustavito always fared worse. When he made a mistake, whether in spelling, arithmetic, or calligraphy, Diana Cuervo's response was always the same: a quick slap on the back of the head along with the rhetorical question "*¿Usted es come mierda?*" the popular Cuban expression—literally shit eater—for stupid. I now realize how easy the rest of us had it. Although I can't remember, I must have met her expectations, for at the end of that year I was promoted to third grade.

SANTERÍA

I t was around that time that I had my first encounter with the spells of *Santería*, or worship of the saints, a practice that has always been prevalent in Cuba, the other islands of the Caribbean, and the northeast sections of Brazil. It was an alternative and clandestine religion developed by African slaves brought to the New World during the eighteenth and nineteenth centuries, and very much a part of Cuban culture, since a large percentage of the population was black. Each saint or *orisha* demanded specific offerings and dispensed punishment in very personal ways. I had heard about the practice, the ceremonies and the different spells, but I had no firsthand experience. Until that day.

A small group of boys and I were walking home from school when we spotted something very unusual in an empty lot, just a few feet from the sidewalk. A dry coconut, painted bright red and white, rested in a small space where the vegetation had been cleared. It was surrounded by a careful arrangement of black feathers and about one hundred bright copper pennies. (At that time, Cuban and American currencies had the same value so American money circulated freely on the island.) We stopped, full of curiosity, and got a little closer.

"Don't anybody touch it!" I shouted as a warning to the group, "This is a *Santería* spell and the saints will punish you if you disturb it." We did not get any closer, but went on our way, not wanting to incur the wrath of the *orishas*.

Later that day, I returned and picked up all the pennies. I had one peso—one dollar—that I could spend in any way I chose. But just in case, in order to protect myself, I only used my left hand. It was common knowledge that if such items were to be handled, to erect a shield, the left hand was the only one permissible. I can't remember how I spent the money but it was probably on candy and soft drinks.

I later talked to my mother about this incident and she was not at all surprised. On that empty lot close to our house—it was several acres in size—many squatters had built their makeshift shacks. Since most of the residents were black, it fully explained their belief in *Santería*. What we had seen that day was just a tangible manifestation of those beliefs. Because this improvised citadel did not have an official name, a postal address or any legal status of any form, my mother simply called it Africa.

Years later, while in high school, a friend and I had the opportunity to attend a *bembé*, or *Santería* ceremony in one of these improvised houses. The occasion was the feast of Saint Barbara, early in December. That Catholic saint had been syncretized as Shangó, one of the *orishas* in the crowded pantheon of the Yoruba religion; her effigy was dressed in bright red and held an avenging sword in her right hand.

I did not know what to expect, but throughout the day the *batá* drums (the three drums used during *Santería* rituals) had been heard, proclaiming the power of the *orishas* and summoning the believers to the ceremony.

Around eight o'clock, making our way through the sinuous path that led from the street to the depths of Africa, we arrived at the small house. Even though it was still early, the tiny living room was very crowded. On the back wall, prominently displayed, there was an altar from which the figure of the saint, surrounded by lit candles in red receptacles, commanded the entire room. Below, resting at her feet, were offerings that the devotees had placed there earlier that day.

I had no idea when the ceremony would begin. After all, there was no formal schedule or a master of ceremonies to set things in motion. Without any apparent signals or preambles, someone began to chant, but not in Spanish. The words were completely incomprehensible to me; I had never heard such sounds before. The language, I would later learn, was Lucumí, one of the African languages that, despite the effort of the Spaniards to suppress it, survived the crossing and had been handed down for generations. Many of those present joined in and soon the single voice had changed into a chorus. I assumed that this was some sort of invocation for the saint to manifest his presence. It was common knowledge that during those sessions, if the *orisha* chose to appear, he would do so by taking over the body of someone in the room.

The chanting became more intense, the sound of the drums louder, and the pungent smell of perspiration permeated everything in the room. Without warning, a middle-aged mulatta with graying hair jumped out in front of the altar as she swayed to the rhythm of the music. The blank expression on her face gave no clue as what was about to happen. Grabbing one of the open bottles of rum, she took a long, generous swig, but did not swallow it. Still swaying to the chanting, she approached the crowd and spat out the rum in a semicircular fashion, thus spraying everyone present. This "blessing" was repeated several times with complete abandon.

"*¡Es el santo!*" someone shouted, but the comment was not

necessary. Everyone knew that the saint was now in the room. The woman kept dancing, but her movements had abruptly changed from fluid to convulsive as if the presence that had momentarily inhabited her was familiarizing himself with the workings of a new body. All the while, she uttered strange, guttural sounds in Lucumí, the same language the devotees had used to summon the *orisha*.

Eventually, all energy spent, she collapsed on the floor. The saint had left the room. I had heard but had not understood; I had watched but had not seen. I might as well have well been deaf and blind, since at that time I was only a curiosity-seeking teenager looking for something different to do on that December evening.

There can be no Cuban culture without the African component. It is reflected in our music, our dances, our food, our speech, and of course, in the racial composition of the population itself. Cuba is a genetic and cultural stew—*un ajiaco genético*. Every Cuban, if not genetically, is at least culturally part African. Throughout the years, I always carried these memories and unanswered questions with me. Eventually, they would take form in my novel *Orisha*, one of the most satisfying in my writing career, since it gave me ample opportunity to explore that aspect of Cuban culture of which I had been a witness during my teens.

CORRUPCIÓN/CORRUPTION

As the school year came to a conclusion, I was hoping that the family would return to Tarará Beach. I had had a great time there and the prospects of being 'asked' to be the ring boy at another wedding were minimal. I envisioned another summer full of carefree fun in the company of my friends.

That summer, however, the family stayed in Pinar del Río. Unbeknownst to me, president Fulgencio Batista had asked my father to become Vice Treasurer of the Republic; consequently, he was busy traveling often to Havana in order to get ready to assume that post. As I said, at that time I did not know why we stayed in Pinar del Río that summer, nor did I question it much. I just assumed that the owner of the house in Tarará had decided to use it himself or perhaps he had sold it. So, Luis and I continued riding our bicycles across the street in Independence Park, visiting friends and collecting comic books.

It was not until much later that I learned that my father had known Batista for a long time, and that he had been offered such an important post under his administration. Although he accepted the position, he only lasted a few months in that capacity.

Before accepting the job, he had met with Batista and told him that the only way he would leave Pinar del Río (and abandon his successful law practice) and come to Havana would be if he were allowed to do his job without any outside interference. Since Batista wanted him there, he agreed readily to my father's terms.

Throughout that summer, and with the aid of Luis Menzoza, a close friend and former member of the secret police, they investigated everyone who worked at the treasury and compiled detailed dossiers of their activities. Many of the people on the payroll were receiving bribes or just stealing from public funds.

Armed with this irrefutable evidence, my father went to see the head of personnel at the Treasury and informed him that as of that date, the people whose names were on the list no longer worked there. They only had two options, either resign or be prosecuted. As a lawyer and former district attorney, he knew he was on firm legal ground.

The weeks passed; the people on the list continued to report to work. Nothing had changed. It was at this point that my father decided to confront Batista himself, to remind him of his promise that there would be no interference with the performance of his duties as Vice Treasurer of the Republic.

It is impossible to say whether Batista thought that his visit was out of the ordinary, but after listening carefully to my father's account that the treasury was full of thieves, he did not seem surprised but simply said, "Luis Alberto, let's not be coy. You are the head man at the treasury, so you should have the lion's share of the money." It was at that point that he knew that nothing was going to change, so he resigned his position immediately and returned to Pinar del Río to continue with his law practice. The one fact that Batista had overlooked was that since my father came from a well-to-do family and made a fair amount of money, the lure of even more wealth was an ineffective incentive to participate in such loathsome activities.

After his abrupt resignation, my father felt obligated to give an explanation, so he went on the radio and publicly denounced Batista's regime as corrupt. Several newspaper articles followed these radio appearances, and by the end of the year he was back in Pinar del Río, as busy as ever practicing law.

The only clue that I had at the time was some newly minted silver coins that my mother gave me. They came in different denominations—10, 25, 50 cents and one peso—and commemorated the centennial of the birth of José Martí (1853-1895), Cuba's greatest patriot. His effigy was prominently displayed on all the coins. My father had brought them from Havana before they were officially issued in 1953. Many years later, as a Christmas gift, I would give my daughter Marisa a key chain that showcased the one peso silver coin as a reminder that her grandfather had briefly held such an important post.

AMIGOS/FRIENDS

With the arrival of autumn—just a word in Cuba, for there is no significant change in the weather—I started to get ready for third grade. Although I had no idea what was in store, the one certainty was that I would not be returning to Diana Cuervo's class. Besides pencils and erasers, my mother bought new notebooks for which she made individual covers with sheets of thin orange construction paper. She labeled each by subject, grade, and my name. Her beautiful handwriting was enhanced by the Parker 51 fountain pen that she had purchased even before I was born.

It was also around that time that she undertook the task of creating a handmade leather briefcase for my father to carry his official documents. After gathering the raw materials (leather, a series of punches, and a brass hammer) she went to work. I suppose that she already had in mind what the end product would look like, but nevertheless it took her a long time to finish it.

Every day, as I came back from school, I would find her sitting at a table, patiently embossing the intricate designs on one side and my father's name on the other. These designs had to be created with the punch and hammer, one blow at a time. Of course, I was curious as to what she had in mind, so I made sure to look closely at her progress as her vision took form. One day, the briefcase was finished and it was absolutely beautiful—a visible and tangible testament to my mother's skill and creativity. My father used it for many years and kept it in his possession until his death in 1962.

These two priceless items (my mother's Parker pen and the leather briefcase) would come into my possession many years later; they were brought out of Cuba by a friend of the family and delivered to my brother Luis, who in turn passed them on to me. Although not very valuable from a monetary point of view, just the fact that both my mother and father touched them so many times carries a significance for which I have no words. They have become family heirlooms that my own children will inherit someday, a solid conduit to their grandparents.

To this day I can't say that I enjoyed school. In front of the Escuela Anexa, there was a small semicircular stone wall, about two feet in height, that held in place the soil for a flowerbed. On its front section, resting on the wall, was a marble block resembling a cemetery headstone; all the particulars about the school had been carved on its surface. Every morning, just before class, I would sit on the wall and lean on the stone, contemplating the day ahead of me. I do not mean to imply that I hated school, but I just believed that there were other more interesting things I could be doing. I attended class, went home, did my homework and then devoted the rest of the days to those activities that really interested me. It was that simple.

Nothing in particular really stands out in my mind about third grade (I can't ever remember my teacher's name), except for two events. The first, although at the time seemed rather inconsequential, would have far more reaching consequences than the second one.

One day during recess, I noticed that another boy's belt buckle had broken and he had difficulty keeping his pants on. I took off my own belt and gave it to him; I suppose my pants fit a little better around the waist. Although we were not really friends, I knew him because we were in the same class. His name was Ezequiel and he had red hair and freckles. He came from a large family of very limited means and he was an orphan; his father had been killed by a driver while operating a horse-drawn cart. They belonged to the Seventh Day Adventist Church and attended services on a regular basis. Of course, at that point in time I did not know these details.

The following day, he brought me the belt back, but I told him to keep it, that I had an extra one at the house. From that day on we talked during recess, and one day he

asked if I had any toys that I did not want. I said that I could not think of anything specific right off hand, but that he was welcome to come home with me after dismissal and I would look.

That day we walked back to my house after leaving school; in my closet I found a baseball glove and gave it to him. I could tell that he was really happy; maybe he did not think I would find anything or that I would not part with any of my possessions. My mother, realizing that his needs went well beyond used toys, asked him to stay for lunch. This accidental visit turned into more frequent ones, and by the end of the school year he came to the house with me on a regular basis to eat lunch, do homework, or just to play.

The second event worthy of mention took place at the end of the school year. This was the time when awards were given during a rather formal ceremony in which the entire student body participated. Besides the medals for good conduct and perfect attendance, the highest honor—*El Beso de la Patria*—or The Kiss of the Motherland, was given to the top student in each grade. You can imagine my surprise when my name was called and the principal handed me a diploma with my name on it and a gold medal with a red, white and blue ribbon, the colors of the Cuban flag.

In my mind I had not done anything special; I just showed up every day, did what was expected of me and went home to engage in those other pursuits that I found a lot more interesting than school. Of course, my parents were quite pleased and they had the diploma framed and hung it in my room where everyone could see it. Years later, reading a journal that my mother kept of my life, I found what in my mind was the best clue as to why that event had taken place. I quote, "Carlitos is like an old man. He comes home from school, changes his clothes, and listens to the episodes of Tanganyka on the radio. Then he reads, studies, or writes until late afternoon when he takes a bath and goes out for a while." It was not so much what I did, but who I was, that caused me to receive the award. It is worthy of note that those activities that my mother mentioned—listening to the radio, reading, writing, studying—have one thing in common. They are rather solitary activities in which one engages the mind and not other people. In other words, those are activities that foster introspection. But at that time I just accepted the award and did not bother to analyze the circumstances. After all, I was just eight years old.

PUERTO ESPERANZA

That summer my parents announced that we would be going to the beach. At first I thought that the house in Tarará had become available again, but then I found out that we were going to Puerto Esperanza, a small fishing village located on the northern coast of Pinar del Río. My father had secured the use of a house there, so we could spend the entire summer swimming and engaging in other outdoor activities. At that point in time, by the way, I had not learned how to swim yet.

The journey from Pinar del Río to Puerto Esperanza took approximately one hour. The road went up in the mountains until it reached the town of Viñales, home of the world-famous valley of the same name, undisputedly one of the most beautiful spots in Cuba, and maybe the entire world. After reaching Viñales, there was a gradual descent towards the coast. About six or seven kilometers before Puerto Esperanza, there was the small town of San Cayetano which could better be described as a cluster of houses.

As we approached the coast, the highway went through the middle of Puerto Esperanza and ended abruptly in front of the sea. By the way, there were no other paved roads in the town. At the very end of the highway, straddling the shore and the sea, stood a huge structure with a wraparound porch. It was a bar call *Mar y Tierra*, or Sea and Land, whose proprietor was a friend of my father. His name was Carlos Carú and he was tall, stocky, and his face was always red as if his blood contained an excessive amount of hemoglobin.

The jukebox of the *Mar y Tierra* worked almost constantly, playing loudly the most popular Cuban songs of that era. Patrons inside the bar could sit at their tables and drink, talk to friends, or dance. The tables on the wraparound porch, I soon learned, were destined for the endless games of dominoes that Cubans love so much.

But this was not the most salient feature of that establishment; there was another, a most incongruous one. In front of the bar, to the left of the entrance, there was a small shrine enclosed in glass with the effigy of the *Caridad del Cobre*, the patron saint of Cuba. Of course, neatly carved in the front glass panel there was a slot so the visitors could make their offerings of pocket change or folded bills. I do not know if this shrine had been erected by the owner of the bar or what happened to the money that was collected. In fact, I did not ask myself these questions until many years later. I just accepted it because it was there.

I can't remember if I was expecting Puerto Esperanza to be something similar to Tarará with its modern houses, paved roads, sandy beaches, and middle-class dwellers but it was nothing like that. Puerto Esperanza was simply a fishermen's village whose inhabitants lived and worked there year around.

The house that my father had secured was yet another surprise, since it had been erected above a warehouse. I had certainly never seen anything like it before. Extending into the ocean, there was a wide pier whose end culminated in a large platform. At one time, long before, ships used to dock there and the goods they delivered were transported onto carts that ran on rails. These carts moved the entire length of the pier and through massive doors that led to a huge warehouse that was built right on the shore. But as I said, that must have been many years ago because the first time we visited the place the pier was in a state of disrepair, making it impossible to reach its end where the loading platform was located. What was left of the rails was nothing but rusty parallel lines leading nowhere, and the warehouse doors had been locked for years. The entire complex had white walls and a red tiled roof. Next to this entrance there was a small stand, where soft drinks, candy and other items were sold. The owner of this enterprise was a tall, thin man with black hair whom everyone called Macho.

Our house, as I said, was built on top of the warehouse so we had to climb a set of exterior stairs and make a ninety-degree turn on a landing before reaching the front porch. The view, however, from that advantageous location, was truly magnificent. One could even see, neatly delineated against the line of the horizon, the different keys so prevalent on the Cuban coastline. Because of its height, and since everything had been whitewashed, my mother immediately called the house *El Palomar,* which roughly translated as The Pigeon House. Teresa, as usual, was to look after us during our stay. My parents went back to Pinar del Río because of work obligations, but came to see us several times a week and on weekends.

Children, rather than looking for faults and shortcomings, only see possibilities, so Luis and I were most excited about the prospect of spending the summer in Puerto Esperanza. We did not make any comparisons between this house and the one where we had stayed two years earlier in Tarará; we just thought of the days ahead and of all the things we would be able to do.

The inside of the house was nothing out of the ordinary. The first room was a huge living room/dining room combination, then a long hallway that led to the kitchen, bathroom, and bedrooms. The furniture and the decoration were rather spartan in nature, but at the time those details were not important, so I did not even notice.

I already mentioned that most of the inhabitants of Puerto Esperanza were locals who lived and worked there all year around, but there was also a small group of people who lived in Pinar del Río and kept summer houses in that town. Among those was my father's younger sister, aunt María Rita, whom we affectionately called Tía Chichí. Her house was right on the highway that led to the sea, about a block up from the *Mar y Tierra*

. That house was painted white with red trim and above the front door there was a wooden plaque labeled "Villa Rosa." I later learned that that summer house had been a Mother's Day present from my father to Rosa, my grandmother. Since Tía Chichí never had any children, throughout the summer she would have different guests, among them my cousins from Havana or Miami.

My cousin Carmen—one of the most beautiful women I have ever seen—lived in Miami since her husband, Clyde, was originally from North Carolina. Their daughters, Alina and June, always came to Cuba for Christmas and during their summer vacation. Even though they were both fluent in Spanish, they often communicated in English with each other or their parents. Luis and I called them *Las Americanitas*—the little Americans—and always looked forward to their visits. For the longest time I had a crush on Alina, but was too shy to say or do anything about it. I just knew that I felt different when she was around and that I missed her when she was not. During the regular year I spent a lot of time thinking about her.

Sometimes, when I visited Havana, I used to imagine that the physical distance between us was diminished and wondered what she would be doing at that particular instant. I also kept in my closet a wooden box with a sliding top (originally it was chalk box) with items that she had handled—a bottle cap, some marbles, etc.—and when I touched them somehow I felt that I was closer to her. On the lid I wrote the letters R.D.A. These initials stood for *Recuerdos de Alina*, or Mementos from Alina, but I never told anyone what those letters meant.

Of course, the main purpose for spending the summer in Puerto Esperanza was to go swimming and engage in other outdoor activities. Unlike Tarará, where white sand could be found right off the shore, there was no easily accessible bathing area in Puerto Esperanza. Every morning we had to get on a rowboat—the owner was one of the locals and his name was Cundo—that would take us to *Los Lirios*, about half a kilometer away. On the way to that bathing area, the bright orange sea stars stood out against the dark background of Sargasso grass below.

Los Lirios was composed of a small wooden platform surrounded by thick mangrove. A set of steps, also made of wood, facilitated on and off access. The bottom of that bathing area was covered in white sand, so one could see everything without any difficulty given the clarity of waters found in the Caribbean. It was a nice morning ritual; after about an hour, we made the journey back to Puerto Esperanza to engage in other pursuits.

One of the most unforgettable experiences of my life I witnessed at *Los Lirios*. The spot was so peaceful, so removed from everything that no one ever thought anything could happen there.

That day was no different from any other; we had gotten into

Cundo's boat, as we did every day, traveled the half-mile, and were simply enjoying the ocean in the company of family and friends. Shattering the quiet, we heard the sound of an engine. It came on so unexpectedly that right away I knew that it was not a boat. Besides, the sound came from above, not from sea level.

Within seconds we spotted a small plane leisurely circling the bathing area. I do not recall if the pilot or his passenger were trying to wave to us or if they were just trying to show off. What I do remember is that with every successive pass, the plane came closer and closer to the water. The plane would climb, make a circle, and fly again over *Los Lirios*, diving and then quickly gaining altitude again in a sharp maneuver. Somehow, I sensed that something dreadful was about to happen. It was during the third or fourth pass that the pilot miscalculated the distance, or he pulled on the up control just a second too late. As soon as the tip of the propeller touched the water the engine stalled. Then, nose first, the plane began to sink slowly into the water.

We were all stunned but by that time Cundo was already rowing in the direction of the spot where the plane had sunk. Although only about twenty feet deep, it was enough to swallow the plane and cause everyone on board to drown. The pilot had managed to extricate himself from his seat belt, and his head was above water. His wife—we did not know this at the time—had not been so lucky; she had been pulled down with the plane, still strapped to her seat.

Cundo did not hesitate. From his boat he dove into the water, trying to bring up the woman trapped below. After a short while he came up for air. Not being able to unbuckle the seat belt, this time he dove back into the water with a knife he had retrieved from the boat. This second attempt was successful, but as the woman was pulled onto the boat, it was evident that she was bleeding. During his desperate attempt to cut the safety belt, Cundo had inadvertently also made some superficial cuts on her arms.

She was rushed as quickly as possible to Puerto Esperanza where one of the local doctors administered first aid. Afterwards, she was taken to Pinar del Río in an ambulance where she could receive more comprehensive care and recuperate at the hospital. Although I knew that she survived, I never found out any of the particulars of that episode or the reason for the odd and reckless behavior of the pilot.

About a month later, the wreckage of the plane was dragged over the ocean floor until it came to rest about three or four hundred feet from the shore, right in front of the spot where the highway ended. Long and thick ropes were attached to the aluminum fuselage and just about everyone in town, including myself, began to pull until what was left of the plane emerged from the water. The material that had once covered the wings and fuselage was gone; all that remained was the metal skeleton. For years afterwards that bare frame was displayed in an empty lot close to the water, a grim reminder of that tragic event that had taken place on that beautiful morning at *Los Lirios*.

The other memorable event of that summer was a lot less dramatic, but a lot more useful: I learned how to swim. As I mentioned earlier, there was no bathing area in Puerto Esperanza, hence the trips to *Los Lirios*. Of course, we could not be happy with just an hour in the morning, so we had to improvise. It was possible to walk on that old pier, despite the cracked or missing planks, about one hundred and fifty feet. Beyond that point a section had collapsed, leaving a gap between that truncated end and the loading platform farther out to sea.

This particular section of the pier was used by the locals—including Cundo—to tie their boats when they were not in use. It was also used by the local boys as a swimming spot. Being as close as it was to the house—a five-minute walk—it was only logical that I should join them. In retrospect, I realize that I never found out their real names since they all went by their nicknames—El Niño, Papirola, Cacique, Mosquito—but we became good friends and I looked forward to seeing them every summer.

Since these kids could not pay Cundo to take them to *Los Lirios*, they had to make do with whatever was available, so they used the end of the old pier as their private swimming spot at whatever time was convenient for them. Little by little I got more confident until I could float indefinitely. From there it was just a matter of time until I mastered the breast stroke, and by the end of that summer I felt completely at ease in the water.

Besides the time spent in the ocean, we also rode our bicycles all over town. Since there was only one paved road, cars seldom ventured onto the side streets, so there was really no danger from traffic. Sometimes entire bicycle caravans would just materialize, and for hours would explore the remotest areas of Puerto Esperanza, going as far as the line of mangroves that grew along the ocean would allow us. During those days we would often return home covered in mud because of the many potholes that were still full of water from recent rains. But it did not really matter; we would simply change into our bathing suits and dive in the ocean rather than taking a shower.

We always rose early, and after a quick breakfast of *café con leche* and hot toast we got ready to start the day. The porch of the house, because of its height, gave us an unobstructed view of the beach below. I always thought that the ocean appeared to be a very smooth and endless sheet of glass rather than water. This illusion was disrupted occasionally when a fish would unexpectedly break the surface and dive again, leaving in its wake a series of tenuous ripples. But it was more than just the stillness of the ocean; the silence of the hour also seemed to reflect an overall sense of absolute quiet, as if the very machinery of time had come to a halt and we were suspended in a remote region where nothing was ever destined to move or evolve.

As the sun increased its parabola in the sky, so did the activity around the pier. The hoarse sound of distant diesel engines coming to life traveled across the surface of the water letting everyone know that another day had begun; muffled voices of the fishermen were also heard and the first group of early risers, on their way to their jobs, showed up at the pier.

Another day had begun, offering us an array of endless possibilities along with the illusion that life would never change, and further, that we would never change and would be able to enjoy indefinitely this carefree existence.

That summer the construction of a new pier was started. Since the number of visitors and permanent summer vacationers had been steadily increasing, the expense and effort was justified. Our house—fortunately, I thought—was right smack between the old and new piers. Every day we watched the workmen drive the pylons into the ocean floor and often wondered if they had any idea of what they were trying to accomplish.

Those days were so easy that we completely lost track of time and often we did not know—or care—what day it was. Before we knew it, the summer was over and it was time to return to Pinar del Río to start another school year. Although the town of Puerto Esperanza was inferior in every way to Tarará, I loved the time spent there since we had absolute freedom and the days were ours to do as we pleased.

This coastal town, including the *Bar Mar y Tierra*, would later become the setting for many of my short stories and for my novella *Hubris*. To this day, I have nothing but fond memories of Puerto Esperanza and often wonder what it would be like to return after all these years.

SAN JUAN

After spending the entire summer at the beach, our house in Pinar del Río always seemed bigger than I remembered it and the days more rigid, but getting back into the routine was not that difficult a task. I did not even mind getting up early, putting on my uniform, and walking to school.

Besides the occasional trip to Havana to visit relatives and the summers in Puerto Esperanza, Luis and I often visited the nearby town of San Juan y Martínez. Amancio, one of my father's clients, owned a farm there and he was always glad when we spent the day at his place. He was tall, slender, and had gray hair. He was probably in his mid-fifties or early sixties. His wife Veneranda was a few years younger and, just as her husband, was always happy to see us come; she often wore bright dresses and had a liking for talcum powder which she used profusely around her neck. Perhaps they liked our visiting their house because they had no children of their own, but that is just speculation on my part.

The one trait about Amancio that we always had to keep in mind was that he was very hard of hearing. Someone told me that once, while talking on the telephone, lightning had struck the line and that the loud noise had damaged his ear drum but I cannot affirm that this is a true story. Needless to say, I never asked him.

The trip from Pinar del Río to San Juan took about forty minutes by bus and it cost less than one peso. Luis and I would walk to the bus station, get on the appropriate bus, and prepare to spend the day at Amancio's farm. This was not difficult to do since his house was within walking distance from the bus station. After all, San Juan was a small town in the heart of tobacco country where everyone knew everyone else.

Amancio's house, as were most houses in San Juan, was smaller than those found in Pinar del Río. From the street to his front porch there was a concrete walk that straddled a ditch that carried rain water to the nearby river.

Two events in particular that took place during our visits stand out in my mind. The first was rather trivial, while the second one could have had a lot more disastrous consequences.

Behind Amancio's house, along the path that led to the river, there was a medium size pigpen. There is nothing strange about this fact. After all, this was a farm where all sorts of animals were kept. Growing next to the pigpen was a robust plum tree and as Luis and I walked by, we always picked some plums. They were yellow and very juicy. But it just so happened that one of the branches—the one that had the most fruit—reached over the pigpen, thus making it completely inaccessible. As the plums ripened, they fell off the tree directly into the pigpen below. I thought this was a waste; I wanted the plums for myself.

Having reached this conclusion, all I needed was a way of gathering the fruit. The most logical and obvious way was to climb the tree, crawl along the branch, pick the fruit and toss them beyond the reach of the pigs below. Then I would gather them and eat them. What could be easier?

The tree itself was not very tall, so I had no difficulty reaching the point where the trunk forked into the different branches.

Once there, after resting momentarily on one of the forks, I continued on my quest. The one fact that I had failed to consider, however, was that as the branch grew farther away from the tree, its girth diminished proportionally. But I would not be deterred from my goal, so I continued my slow progress along the branch, inching my way to its end. Just as I was about to reach out for the first cluster of plums, the weight of my body exceeded the support of the branch and it unexpectedly swayed downward towards the pigpen below. I tried to hold on, but by then all sense of balance had been lost and I found myself in the midst of the squealing and grunting pigs. I had not been hurt because I landed in the thick and soft bed of mud and excrement. All my clothes, of course, had to be washed while I took a bath and licked my psychological wounds. What made this incident even more humiliating, in my view, was that as I fell off the branch, all the ripe fruit was shaken off the tree and had landed in the pigpen to be hastily consumed by the animals. All my work had been for nothing.

The second incident took place during a different visit. As usual, Luis and I arrived in the morning and spent some time with Amancio and Veneranda. For lunch we usually had a piece of very thin steak that she cooked with onions, white rice, and plantains; the dessert consisted of guava shells in syrup with a slice of cream cheese. A typical simple and delicious Cuban meal.

That afternoon, as we had done so many times before, we decided to go for a swim. The path that led to the river, as I stated before, was behind the house and it extended about a quarter of a mile past the plum tree. This was one of those occasions when Amancio did not let us go wandering around on our own; he was responsible for our safety so he always came with us.

The river was not very wide but its bed got progressively

deeper and the water flowed with more speed and force as one approached its center. As we got closer, we could hear the sound of the water rushing around the boulders that protruded in the middle of the stream; the banks were covered with multicolored stones that the force of the current had smoothed out and polished over countless years. We often tossed the flatter stones, while putting a spin on them, to make them skip on the surface of the water.

As Luis and I took off our clothes, Amancio sat on one of the boulders next to the bank. The water, as always, was clear and warm; we were both familiar with the swimming spot so we did not hesitate and got in within minutes. The same smooth stones that covered the banks were also found at the bottom of the river, and they provided a firm footing as we delved deeper into the current towards the center of the stream.

At this point I don't know if I was somehow distracted, but above the sound of the water forcing its way around the rocks I heard Luis crying out for help as the current carried him away. Whether he had lost his footing or had simply gone too far into the deeper part of the river, I will never know. Even though Amancio was there, still sitting on the rock, he could not hear the cries for help as Luis was swept away by the current.

I did not hesitate, but immediately went after him, using the swimming skills I had acquired in Puerto Esperanza. About twenty or thirty yards downstream I caught up to him and managed to grab one of his arms. At this point, of course, we were both being swept away by the force of the water. Fortunately, and still holding on to each other, we managed to reach one of the boulders that was anchored to the bed of the river. From there, after resting a few moments, we swam to the bank about fifty yards from where Amancio was still sitting on the rock. He never found out what had happened and we never told anyone; we just realized that the river was potentially dangerous and that we had to be careful. But this was not our last visit to Amancio's farm; we would return many other times, especially after we acquired our BB guns, but that would not be until years later.

COMUNIÓN/COMMUNION

The prospect of starting fourth grade neither thrilled me nor annoyed me; it was something that had to be done, that is all. The school had not changed; the almond trees that lined the sidewalk were still there, so was that marble slab that I used as a back support while I waited for the doors to open for the day. My mother, as she did every year, had carefully made covers for all my notebooks. Using her Parker fountain pen and incomparable handwriting, she labeled each with the subject matter and my name.

Most of the students in the class were the ones from the previous year, including Ezequiel, the boy to whom I had given a belt and a baseball glove a few months before. I resumed my friendship with him; he kept coming around often, and usually stayed for lunch.

Life resumed its usual course; I went to school, did my homework as soon as I came home, and then spent the rest of the day reading, riding my bicycle in the park across the street, or playing with the other boys from the neighborhood. I also listened to the radio on a regular basis—we had no television at this time—and I particularly enjoyed serial programs that broadcast a new episode every day. There was one show in particular, *El Secreto del Dios Tambú* (The Secret of the Tambú God) that soon became my favorite. As was often the case, it

68

portrayed a confrontation between good and evil. The setting was equatorial Africa and there was a frantic search for a coveted golden statue of the god. Everyone knew that the statue was at the bottom of a lake, but so far no one had been able to dive to such depths to retrieve it.

Sakiri el Malayo (Sakiri the Malaysian), a portrayal of pure evil, aided by his henchman Colmillo (Fang), would force the natives to dive into the lake. Sakiri spoke Spanish with an accent, so as to make the character more convincing. I have no idea if this was a correct Malaysian accent, but it really did not matter since it set him apart from the rest of the characters. Let's not forget that radio is an entirely auditory medium and as such, every device had to be used to stimulate the imagination of the audience.

Against their will, the natives dove into the lake but invariably had to come up for air, unable to reach the statue of the god Tambú. Sakiri was not happy; failure was always punishable by death. Here is where Colmillo came in. The unfortunate native was made to run; then Colmillo, who wore around his wait a sash with countless knives, would throw one at him. As he ran, the man always uttered the same plea: *"¡No Colmillo, todavía no, todavía no!"* (Not yet, Colmillo, not yet!) Then there would be a scream as the knife lodged itself into the nape of the man's neck. Afterwards, loud laughter of satisfaction followed by a frightful statement: *"¡Colmillo nunca falla!"* (Colmillo never misses!).

As you can imagine, I was glued to the radio every afternoon following Sakiri's and Colmillo's evil deeds as they desperately searched for the golden statue. Besides my other personal interests and activities, I really looked forward to this radio program. After all, I could hardly wait until such absolute evil was finally eradicated from the face of the earth, for I knew that the forces of Good would eventually triumph and bring them to justice. I wanted both Sakiri and Colmillo to suffer a painful, lingering death so they would get a taste of their own medicine.

It was around that time that my mother decided that it was time for my first communion. Although not particularly religious—I never saw my parents attending church—my family (as most Cuban families) followed those prescribed Catholic rites of passage that every child had to complete. Of course, this was not so simple. Before receiving communion, there was a period of preparation and one of the requirements was the successful completion of catechism classes. All this work culminated on that special day when the first communion was received.

At first, I was not opposed to the idea since it was something that everyone did, just like going to school and doing homework. Then my mother gave me the specifics of the class schedule. Catechism classes, it just so happened, were held at the exact same time as when *El Secreto del Dios Tambú* was broadcast. I was totally dismayed. I felt that by listening to the episodes I was giving my moral support to the forces of Good; I wanted to witness (at least audibly) Sakiri's defeat and Colmillo's downfall.

Of course, the decision had been made; I was already enrolled in what I considered to be a blatant intrusion into my personal time. I even considered that the forces of Evil were secretly conspiring against me. There was no escape; I had to make the best of a bad situation.

Catechism classes were held at the private home of an old lady whose name I have long since forgotten. Her house was located about four blocks away, on Luz Zaldívar Street. By the time I arrived for the first class, a group of boys and girls was already there. Just as I did, they had their small catechism books in hand. I had no idea what to expect, but I was not happy. I kept thinking of Sakiri and Colmillo, and of all the evil deeds they were perpetrating during my absence.

As it turned out, catechism classes were not classes at all, but a series of programmed exercises of memory. The lady in charge would assign a prayer or a passage from the booklet to be memorized. The following day, we stood in line and recited what she had assigned the day before. Those who reproduced it to her satisfaction—that is to say, flawlessly—could go home. Those who stumbled or could not come up with the right words were sent to the back of the line, to review the work and try again when everybody else was done.

I soon realized that I could work this system to my advantage. Memorizing the prayers was not a problem—I have been blessed, or cursed, with an excellent memory—but minimizing the time spent there was. I solved this problem with a very simple strategy: I showed up early, before any of the other students came. That meant, of course, that I was first in line and while I waited I had some time to review the assignment.

When the door opened, I was ready. Everyone sat down, except me; the prayers had to be delivered standing up in front of the group. I closed my eyes, so as not to be distracted, and recited the prescribed words in a very clear, deliberate manner. The old lady was pleased, for she praised me and then told me that I could go home. I did not linger, but literally ran the four blocks to my house and, still panting, turned on the radio. I managed to catch the last ten minutes of the program; it was better than nothing at all.

The next day at school during recess, my friends would bring me up to date on the wicked deeds that Sakiri and Colmillo had carried out the previous day. My mother, of course, was pleased with my progress but at the same time realized that I was still not happy with the arrangement. This went on for a while; I showed

71

up early, said the prayers, and ran home to listen to the tail end of *El Secreto del Dios Tambú*.

Towards the end of the catechism course, the instructor met individually with the parents to deliver a progress report; she alone decided whether the children were ready or not to receive their first communion. On the day she met with my mother, the old instructor was full of praises about my performance and attitude. "I think Carlitos is special," she finally concluded.

"Really? How so?" asked my mother, curious as to what she had to say.

"I believe that your son may have a budding vocation. He is always the first one to arrive, he really concentrates when he says his prayers, and he does not linger afterwards to socialize with the other children. Could we be in the presence of a neophyte?" she asked rhetorically.

My mother, of course, could hardly contain her laughter; she was well aware of how annoying those classes were to me. That hour had been reserved for the worship of the god Tambú; anything else was an unwelcome intrusion.

"Only time will tell," she answered, "but thank you for making me aware of this situation. I will certainly keep an eye on him."

This seemingly trivial incident, and the instructor's mistaken conclusion, became the seed from which my novel *The Neophyte* would sprout so many years later. As I wrote that book I kept thinking about my mother laughing, and how much she would have enjoyed that particular tale.

First communion took place without any problems. We were all dressed in white, had a ribbon tied to the left arm, and held a book of prayers with white-gloved hands. As was customary, a professional photograph was taken in front of a crucifix and small, parchment-like souvenirs were printed and distributed to family and friends.

What I remember most about that day was the taste (or maybe I should say lack of taste) of the communion wafer. I found it strangely appealing, not in a religious way, but as something that pleased my palate. Right away I embarked on a quest to secure a supply of those round and delicate disks. First, I asked my mother but she said that, to her knowledge, no store in town sold them. I then checked with the local bakeries, a logical move, I thought, but was also unsuccessful. No one seemed to know who made them, or where they could be bought.

Then I had the idea of going to the house where the bishop lived. If anyone knew, he would. After all, the church had to have a steady supply to satisfy the need of parishioners as they went to communion every week.

Although I had not been there since my baptism—an event of which I had no recollection—I knew exactly where the building was. Its impressive and august carved double doors subtly announced the ecclesiastical nature of the enterprise within. Using the massive brass knocker, I made my presence known. Within seconds the door opened and a man, with a curious look on his face, asked about the purpose of my visit.

Needless to say, the bishop was much too busy to see me, so I explained to him the nature of my quest for the unconsecrated hosts. He listened patiently, then proceeded to explain that those wafers were made especially for the church, and that they were not available to the general public. I have no idea if he had ever heard the same request before but it did not matter. I returned home, somewhat disappointed, since I knew that there was no way for me to taste the unleavened bread unless I went back to communion, but I never did.

FUNERAL

The other memorable event that year, far more serious than my not being able to listen to my radio show, happened unexpectedly. Ezequiel's mother died. I do not know whether she had been ill or if it happened without warning. All I remember is that he was absent from school and that the teacher informed the class. A collection was taken and we all went to his house wearing our school uniforms. Although he frequented my house almost daily, I had never visited his.

The maze of streets leading to his home was unpaved and all the houses looked similar. This place was known as *Cuatro Caminos*, a shantytown that had sprung up and was located on the outskirts of the town. The house was small and was constructed from clapboard, and the surface of the porch was not tiled, but showed a simple concrete slab. Inside the living room was dark and pictures of family members hung on the walls, overlooking the humble furnishings.

Pepe Jiménez, one of our classmates, delivered the money we had collected to one of the members of the family, probably an older brother. We stayed for a while, then the teacher led the class out of *Cuatro Caminos*. I understood then why Ezequiel had never invited me to visit his house. Even though we attended the same school and played the same games, we lived in two very different worlds. He came from a very large family whose

74

members had never gone beyond the elementary grades in school and, as of that day, both his parents were gone.

In contrast, my family was small, my parents were professionals and, most importantly, they were still alive. The word that came to my mind when I thought of him at that moment was *desamparado*—someone who has been left without shelter or protection of any kind. I do not mean to imply that he no longer had a place to live, food to eat, or clothes to wear. His older brothers would see to that. What he had lost was irreplaceable; there is no substitute for the love, psychological protection, and tender touch that only a mother can provide. Even as a young boy I knew that. Just a few short years later after leaving Cuba and finding myself alone in a third-rate Miami hotel, faced with nothing but an uncertain future, I would experience that unfathomable sense of loss that Ezequiel must have felt at that time, but to a lesser degree since my parents were still alive. Without a doubt, the fact that these events happened so early in his life, when he had so little control over his own destiny, must have left an indelible imprint that he would always carry with him. There was no way possible for me to even begin to imagine what he must have felt. As I said, we attended the same school and played the same games but ultimately, we lived in different universes where different rules applied. Many years later, ironically, it would be Ezequiel who would place a long-distance telephone call to inform me of my own mother's death.

ANATOMÍA/ANATOMY

B ut life inexorably goes on, and by the conclusion of
the school year I was no longer thinking about these
things. By then I was looking forward to going back to
Puerto Esperanza and spending the summer without any school
obligations or time schedules. As she had done the previous
summer, Teresa would accompany us and our parents would
come to see us several times a week.

So we made the trek from Pinar del Río in my father's '52 Ford,
going through the different towns on that road that eventually
ended on the northern coast of the province. As we drove into
Puerto Esperanza, I did not notice any changes. The houses on
either side of the road looked the same; the hardware store was
still there; the skeleton of the plane we had pulled out of the
ocean the previous summer still sat on the empty lot. And of
course, the *Mar y Tierra* bar still beckoned its customers with
its lively music and games of dominoes. Next to the bar, the
small glass shrine to the *Caridad del Cobre* eagerly welcomed the
monetary offerings that the believers deposited through the slot
on the front glass pane.

As we walked past the small shrine towards the rusty rails
that once connected the now empty warehouse to the loading
platform at the end of the old pier, I noticed that Macho's stand
was gone. But I soon realized that he had simply relocated—he

now had a small trailer—next to the entrance of the new pier, which by then had been completed. Besides the usual candy and soft drinks, he also sold fried fish that was brought to him by the local boys. He also had a radio that played popular music uninterruptedly all day long.

The new pier, as far as I know, had been the brainchild of those vacationers who had summer homes in the town. Although narrower and not as long as the old one, it was a lot more modern and it also reflected the purpose of its construction: to serve people and not to move cargo. At its very end there was an open structure with a red-tiled roof and wooden benches around its perimeter. There was also a slide that led into the water.

Four different bathing areas, at different depths, had been created. Each had its own set of steps leading into the water. The builders had also had the foresight of enclosing the entire area within a tight wooden fence whose sturdy poles protruded about two feet from the surface of the water. The public could swim and enjoy the ocean without any fears of an unpleasant encounter with large marine animals. Beyond the deepest bathing area, there were two trampolines built at different heights. After the completion of this new pier, the daily trips to *Los Lirios* became a thing of the past. Our house, fortunately for us—I said this before—was located between the old and new piers, so everything was readily accessible.

We did not waste any time. After climbing the stairs on the face of the building and going into the house, we put on our bathing suits right away, came downstairs, and walked to the very end of the new pier; we examined the different bathing areas and made comments all along about how nice everything had turned out. After exploring its entire length we went swimming, starting with the bathing area where the water just reached the waist, and eventually moving to the deepest one where our feet could not reach the bottom.

That second summer we had brought with us diving masks, so not only could we swim at our leisure, but also explore the bottom of the ocean as long as our breath would allow us. The best day for diving was Monday since most of the visitors to Puerto Esperanza came on Sundays and always lost something in the water. I remember finding coins of different denominations, cheap jewelry, and even a set of dentures! I placed these items in a cardboard box that I called 'My Treasure Chest.' For a ten-year old boy, this was truly paradise; I had absolute freedom to do anything I wanted and I soon renewed the friendships with the local boys that I had met the previous summer.

Since we had no TV (We had, however, an old radio that we used to listen to the serial novels that were broadcast throughout the year.) —nor did we want one—to pass the time and make a little money we started a kite business. The thin paper, glue, string, and reeds necessary for their manufacture were readily available at the local stores. Using the dining room table, we let our imaginations run wild and constructed kites of different colors and sizes. Later, they were displayed outside and sold for ten cents apiece. Of course, there were always boys who did not find exactly what they were looking for, so we would make them a kite to their specifications for an extra five cents. A very popular design was a skull with crossbones above the name of the owner. From time to time we also made a *cometa*, or oversized kite, but those were more expensive and did not sell well since they were not as nimble in the air as the regular ones.

In the afternoons, after eating lunch in the porch that over-looked the ocean, we would fly the kites; it was not until that hour that the wind picked up. Some of the boys liked doing it from the shore; others did it from the new or old piers. Unexpectedly, the blue sky would be spotted with myriad colorful designs that combined into a dazzling kinetic display. But this activity went beyond just flying the kites. Attached to their tails, every two feet or so, we affixed razor blades, thus turning them into aerial weapons. We would maneuver the kites for hours, adjusting their height and position so the tails would coincide with someone else's string. Then, with a quick pull, the razor blades would carry out their mission and sever the anonymous string. The kite, momentarily deprived of the guide transmitted from below, would sway from side to side, aimlessly carried by the afternoon breeze until it fell into the ocean. Everyone had fun during these aerial battles and it was good for business since the kites had to be replaced.

It was during that second summer in Puerto Esperanza that we met Totó, one of the local fishermen. Totó worked aboard a *bonitero,* a boat specifically designed for catching *bonito*, a fish similar to tuna, but smaller. He was tall, muscular, and had blondish hair. I now realize that he came around because he liked Teresa but that fact does not really matter. He was lots of fun and always had stories about the fishing trade and the work that he did. The calluses on his hands were a visible corroboration that he had done manual labor all his life and I do not believe that he went very far in school. He also liked to drink and gamble whenever he was on shore, although I never saw him drunk. I suppose that at times he was gone for days since his visits were somewhat sporadic. No one was surprised whenever he showed up, given his irregular schedule.

Through our friendship with Totó, an all-day trip to the more distant keys was organized. Although we had visited *Punta de la Bandera*, the closest of the surrounding keys several times, we had never ventured beyond that point. Besides our family, other people were included, perhaps as a means of defraying the cost of using the *bonitero* for an entire day. After all, diesel fuel had to be purchased and the crew had to be paid.

On the appointed morning, we all huddled on deck and the engines came to life. After undoing the moorings, we were off. As we got away from Puerto Esperanza and the smaller boats that crowded the harbor, the *bonitero* gained speed. Most people stayed on deck, making conversation or looking at the open sea. Totó, of course, took ample advantage of this opportunity to display his vast knowledge of the sea and the fishing trade. Soon we reached *Punta de la Bandera*, the closest of the keys, and given the superior speed of the *bonitero* it was quickly left behind. After a while, I decided to go below since it would be at least two hours before we reached our destination.

I had no idea what to expect, but after going down the rungs of the ladder that led below deck, I found myself in the bowels of the *bonitero*. In the semidarkness I discerned an array of rustic bunk beds that the crew used during their fishing expeditions; the droning sound of the diesel engines was magnified as it reverberated in the hollow cavity. But what really stood out was neither the drab and stark sight of the bunk beds nor the overpowering sound of the engines. The entire enclosure was permeated by an indefinable and overpowering smell that I had never experienced before. Then I realized that it was not a single smell, but a combination of several: raw fish; diesel fuel, and the pungent emanations of the sweaty men who slept there. Since there was a complete lack of ventilation, the smell had become part of the enclosure.

At this point, once my curiosity had been satisfied, the sensible thing would have been to return above deck and join the rest of travelers. But I was not quite done yet. I wanted to know firsthand what it was like to use one the bunk beds, so I walked over to the closest one and lay down. There was no mattress to receive and cushion the body, but just bare boards and no pillow. The bed was hard and uncomfortable, but I did not get up, for as I closed my eyes I could hear the water on the other side of the hull, just inches away, rushing by. It was a strange, soothing sound that incorporated a hypnotic component. Maybe that was how the fishermen managed to sleep in those cramped and smelly quarters. Today, as I evoke that sound, I think of Jason as he had his men tie him to the mast of his ship so he could hear the deadly but alluring song of the sirens. Of course, at the time I was not yet familiar with Greek mythology, so I only sensed the close proximity of the sea and rested below deck with my eyes closed.

An indeterminate time later I went back on deck. We had almost arrived at *Punta Arenas*—Sandy Point—the key that we wanted to visit for the day. As the powerful engines slowed down and were eventually turned off, I could see below the clearest water I have seen in my entire life. Looking at the sandy bottom was like looking through liquid glass. It was a perfect, sunny day with a mild breeze blowing, and the only sound, besides that of the soft waves, was that of the sea gulls. As I looked down again, I saw a very large manta ray slowly hovering over the bottom. It had to be, I thought, at least five feet across. Even though the sight of manta rays was a common one in Puerto Esperanza, the size of this one was highly unusual. It had managed to grow so much because its habitat, being so removed from the influence of humans, had remained undisturbed. It was a sight that I will never forget.

Because of its size, the boat could not come very close to the key, so it was anchored about two or three hundred feet from the shore. The only way to get to the beach was to jump overboard and swim but no one seemed to mind.

Most of the key was covered by a thick proliferation of mangroves where some birds had made their nests. As with most things we did in Puerto Esperanza, there was an absolute freedom to carry out our wishes without interference from adults. I wanted to explore, to find out as much as I could about that place that I imagined, because of its inaccessibility, mysterious and exotic. Even then I realized that I could not get lost if I followed the coastline; eventually I would return to the point of departure.

I cannot recall how long I spent in that pursuit, but the key was really nothing out of the ordinary. As I walked along the beach, I saw seashells, pieces of coral, the spear-like seeds that the mangrove plants drop, and some debris that had washed ashore. In the water there was an occasional starfish—always easily spotted, since their bright orange hue stood out against the white and sandy background—and schools of fish that quickly swam away as they heard me approaching.

I can't remember if I managed to circle the entire key or if I just walked around aimlessly, sometimes following the line of the shore, sometimes trying to follow the random paths that nature itself had created in the thick mangrove. I do remember wondering if anyone could survive alone in such a remote place. Years later, while reading Dafoe's *Robinson Crusoe*, I would recall that particular day on that distant key.

After a while, guided by the sound of voices and laughter, I found myself again at the point where everyone had gathered to have the picnic and go swimming. After eating some of the sandwiches that Teresa had packed, we explored the key some more and went swimming again. By mid-afternoon, it was time to return to Puerto Esperanza, so we swam the short distance to where the *bonitero* was anchored and climbed aboard using the rustic but efficient rungs of the rope ladder that hung from its side.

That night, resting on my cot under the mosquito net and listening to the distant songs that came in through the window mixed with the evening breeze, I recalled the day. As I drifted into sleep, I concluded that it had been a great day, one that had been made possible because of our friendship with Totó, and one that I hoped could be repeated soon.

Every year towards the end of summer, there was a festival in Puerto Esperanza but I never found out what it commemorated. People came from all over and for two days a joyous mood pervaded the entire town. Along the main road, vendors set up their carts, offering the visitors their wares with laudatory words. Food vendors, in particular, took advantage of the occasion to display their culinary art in improvised kitchens that summoned the visitors with their irresistible aroma, the sound of the sizzling fritters or fish frying in deep pans, and the loud exhortations that quickly dissolved into the soft morning breeze.

For the adults there was music, drinking, and dancing.

Formal dancing contests were even organized and cash prizes awarded. They usually took place at the *Mar y Tierra* since that locale had a spacious salon and a loud jukebox. Even though I was only nine or ten, I had full access to the *Mar y Tierra;* at that time there was no set drinking age in Cuba. Who got served and who didn't was left to the discretion of the bartender. I usually had an ice-cold mango juice; I am sure I would not have liked the taste of alcohol.

The *Baile de la Papa*, or Dance of the Potato, was one of the tools

83

used to award the prizes. A potato would be placed between the foreheads of the man and the woman; their objective was to keep it from falling to the ground as they danced. At first, songs with a slow tempo were played—usually nostalgic boleros—so the task was relatively easy. As the competition progressed, so did the tempo of the songs; towards the end only rumbas or mambos were being played. The couples struggled to keep pace with the music, yet keep the potato from falling. From their foreheads it worked its way down to their chests, abdomen and ultimately to the floor of the bar. It was fun, exciting, and everybody had a good time. And of course, Carlos Carú, the owner of the bar, made some money in the process.

But as popular as it was, the dancing contest was not the event that drew the largest crowd. Diving competitions were also staged and they could be watched from the new pier that had been recently completed.

It was here that the more popular events, in my opinion, took place. First, there were the diving competitions for men and women. Contestants came from all over to vie for the cash prizes and to show off their skills. Most of the time, the winners were locals who had grown up next to the ocean and felt as comfortable in the water as they did on land.

But the most popular of all events took place at the end of the day: the *cucaña*. Simply put, the *cucaña* was a pole that extended horizontally about twelve feet from the end of the pier over the water below. At its end, the organizers of the festival had placed a bag that held the cash prize. All one had to do was traverse the entire length of the pole to its end and take possession of the prize. But it was not quite that simple. Its surface had been covered with a thick and sticky layer of grease, making it almost impossible to hold on to it, let alone reach its end. Since there was hardly any friction, the possibility of success was greatly diminished or completely eliminated. Despite the obvious difficulty of the task, the contestants were never in short supply. Lured by the sizable purse, they were more than willing to try.

Some approached the *cucaña* cautiously; they moved off the pier slowly, concentrating on the task at hand and making mental calculations as they slowly placed their bodies on the pole. The public urged them on, shouting words of advice or encouragement as they slowly progressed towards the end, where the money had been placed. More often than not, unable to maintain a grip on the greasy surface, they fell off into the water, splashing loudly.

The next contestant took his place, certain that he would succeed where others had failed, but invariably, because of his jerky movements while trying to reach the end, he fell into the water as well. Everyone realized that this had to do with finesse and not strength. Those who succeeded did not move spasmodically but rather they slithered along the length of the pole until reaching the end and grabbing the prize. It was not until then that they purposely fell into the water, surrounded by the cheers and applause of the public.

It is clear that all these activities were aimed at the adults who lived or visited Puerto Esperanza; children were allowed to watch, but not to participate. That does not mean, of course, that the children were left out of the festival.

The organizers, fully cognizant that everyone should be in-cluded, had scheduled a series of events specifically geared towards the young. They consisted mostly of different types of races: sack races, where teams of two placed a leg—the right and the left—in a burlap bag and then had to run towards the finish line. I participated in one such race and my partner and I ended up rolling on the ground due to our lack of coordination. It was certainly not as simple as it looked.

The egg races were also popular. Each contestant held a spoon between his teeth and an egg was placed in the bowl. Once the word "go" was given, one had to move as quickly as possible towards the finish line. Of course, if one moved too fast or failed to keep the spoon in a completely horizontal position, the egg would immediately fall to the ground and break. I never managed to finish one of these races, let alone win it.

But my favorite, by far, was the bicycle race. The finish line was at the end of the road by the *Mar y Tierra*, and the start was farther up the road, about one hundred meters away. The purpose of this race, however, was not to be the first to reach the finish line, but to be last. The rules were simple: one could not go backwards and the feet could not touch the ground. Braking was allowed. Although I never won one of these races either, I always participated because it was so much fun.

Just imagine, a bunch of kids on their bicycles, trying desperately to go as slowly as possible without losing their balance, moving backwards, or placing their feet on the ground. A repeat winner of this contest was Papirola, a black kid and local resident who had one of the most dilapidated bicycles I have ever seen. His technique involved moving the handlebars very quickly from side to side, making his bicycle almost stand still. I don't know how he did it, but he was always the last to reach the finish line.

It was a memorable weekend since there was something for everybody. Come Monday morning, everything was back to normal: the crowds had disappeared and the town appeared, in comparison, almost deserted as it returned to its slow, almost lethargic pace.

But not all my experiences in Puerto Esperanza had to do

with outdoor activities or sharing my time with friends. As I already mentioned, Tía Chichí also spent the summer there. *Las Americanitas* and Tutico, another cousin from Havana, stayed at her house when they came to visit.

Tía Chichí had two people in her employ. One was Alberto, a black man who worked for her year-round and also came from Pinar del Río. He had been her cook for as long as I could remember and would stay by her side until her death many years later. The other was a young woman—probably in her mid-twenties—who worked for her whenever she came to Puerto Esperanza. She was thin, at least by Cuban standards, and went about her duties quietly and efficiently. In my mind, there was really nothing remarkable about her. The room she occupied was not connected to the house, but constructed off a small backyard. It was a typical room destined for servants; she was close without actually sharing the same living space as the family.

One day, during one of my visits, Alberto asked me what I thought was a very strange question. "Are you coming to the anatomy classes this afternoon?" he said. School was not in session, and I had never heard of such classes. "Come back after lunch," he said, "Tutico and José Ignacio will be there too. Just keep it to yourself." José Ignacio was a classmate whose parents had a retail business in Pinar del Río and a summer house right next door to Tía Chichí's in Puerto Esperanza. He was my age and had an older sister named Gloria whom everybody thought was beautiful. They were not wrong. At the time I did not realize that he had not mentioned either Gloria or *Las Americanitas* but just the boys.

That afternoon, after lunch, I returned to Tía Chichí's house. As usual, everybody was taking a nap at that time of the day, so the house appeared to be deserted. Alberto appeared, and sensing my puzzlement, just pointed to the door that led to the backyard of the house then he disappeared.

Tutico and José Ignacio were already there since they did not have to walk any distance at all; they seemed to be as intrigued as I was. The young woman who worked for my aunt appeared in the threshold of her door and beckoned us to come in. Since there was no place to sit down, we just stood, waiting, but not knowing exactly for what.

"Today is the start of anatomy class," she said, adopting a professorial tone, "Make sure to pay attention."

This situation was even more puzzling than I thought; I was thinking of a regular classroom, with a textbook and a chalkboard, but this was quite different. I am sure the other boys were as fascinated as I was but we did not have to wonder long.

"These are the ears," she said while raising her hands and pointing directly to the spot where her colorful earrings hung. "These are the eyes," she said in the same tone, as if she were imparting a most vital piece of information, as she pointed to her eyes.

This went on for a while; she enumerated and then pointed out the plainly visible parts of her anatomy. Eventually, of course, she ran out of things to mention. "And these," she continued in the same professorial tone, as she pointed to them, "are the breasts."

I think that at this point we all thought that she was going to continue enumerating the other parts of the body—hips, legs, etc., as she pointed them out. We could not have been more wrong, for she started to unbutton her blouse very slowly and carefully, with deliberate movements reminiscent of those of an archeologist about to uncover a priceless artifact.

We were both speechless and mesmerized. We could not take our eyes off her. After a moment, the blouse was discarded on the nearby bed. But she was not done yet. Cognizant that she had our full attention, she reached behind her back, carefully undid her bra, and allowed it to slide off her arms.

This was the highlight of her anatomical lecture; she allowed us to look at our leisure, conscious that we had never seen the bare breasts of a woman before, especially so close and for so long. No one said or did anything; we were much too intimidated to ask any questions, let alone reach out and touch those breasts that were being offered for our unobstructed inspection and unadulterated delight. After a while, once she was convinced that we had seen enough, she put her clothes on and dismissed the 'class.'

I never mentioned this to anyone; no explanations were needed for me to realize that I had participated in a secret and forbidden ceremony that would have dismayed my parents. Or maybe not. This was my first glimpse into the culture of *machismo*, so prevalent in Cuban society and Latin America in general. Boys were expected to become men, and one of the most important lessons was to know women. Without a doubt, we were on the right path. This incident was the first in a chain that would culminate years later, while still attending high school, in my first sexual encounter with a woman.

For girls, the situation was the complete opposite. Just imagine if Alberto had conducted the same 'classes' for Gloria and *Las Americanitas*. If found out, he surely would have been beaten to a pulp by their fathers and then thrown in jail. But as I said, we were boys and certain patterns of behavior were not only condoned, but expected.

I was not shocked by this incident. I fact, I looked forward to the next 'class,' secretly hoping that during that second session the 'instructor' would reveal all that she had omitted during the first meeting. That second encounter, however, never took place. The summer ended and we returned to Pinar del Río to start the new school year.

ALBINO

That fall I did not return to the Escuela Anexa. Right across from our house, on the other side of Independence Park and next to a convent of nuns, was a private school called Academia Valella. The owner and principal was señor Valella, a tall, balding man who usually wore *guayabera* shirts and was well-liked by everyone. The uniforms, rather than dark-blue pants and tie with a white shirt, were brown and beige. The students were also issued a *Carnet de Identidad*, complete with a photograph, which identified them as students of the school. Although I was never given an explanation—nor did I ask for one—why we had switched schools, I suspect that my parents were looking ahead to that day when I would have to take a general examination to be admitted to the program of *bachillerato*, the equivalent of the American high school. Academia Valella offered smaller classes, probably better-paid teachers, and a more rigorous program of study.

By then, Ezequiel was not only having lunch with us every day but he also occasionally spent the night. Somehow it was decided that he should also attend the same school. I am certain that my parents must have spoken to the older brother who had legal custody to get his approval. They also must have mentioned that, since Ezequiel's family did not have any money, they would take care of the tuition that had to be paid monthly.

So, we started out the academic year at a new school and tried to adapt as quickly as possible. There were two sessions during the day, morning and afternoon, and a two hour recess in between for lunch. Of course, we just had to walk across the park so we always had plenty of time. I do not recall classes being any more difficult but they were smaller.

That Christmas season, as we did every year, we put up a small tree, decorated it with ornaments, and also set up a nativity scene by its base. I still remember the figures of the three wise men, Melchor, Gaspar, and Baltazar. My favorite was Gaspar, not because he was in any way different from the other two, but because I just liked his beard.

That season, on the night of January 5th, Ezequiel stayed the night. This was the one night that every Cuban child looked forward to throughout the year, since on the morning of the 6th the three wise men would leave their presents for them.

Luis and I were used to getting lots of toys and we always made a list of the things we would like to have. That year we had asked for new bicycles since the ones we had were now too small for us. Rather than leaving the presents next to the tree, the three wise men were in the habit of leaving them right in our rooms by the feet of the beds. That morning we woke up earlier than usual, and besides several small presents, we also found the new bicycles. Ezequiel had one too, and just as many presents as Luis and me. From the very beginning my parents did not want to make any distinctions; we were all treated equally.

There is no way for me to know what he felt that morning since I had never been in his situation before. The one certainty is that he was ecstatic with all his presents, especially with his brand-new red bicycle. Of course, right after breakfast we took them across the street and rode in the park for many hours.

There were many other children there, all with some new toy that the three wise men had left at their houses the night before.

Besides the presents that he received that year, Ezequiel had also found a girlfriend at Academia Valella. It was nothing serious, of course, but part of the rites of passage that every Cuban boy had to observe on his way to becoming a man. They would see each other during recess at school and sometimes at the park.

Later that year, for Valentine's Day, she gave him an embroidered handkerchief that she had carefully sprinkled with the perfume that she wore. Ezequiel did not use this handkerchief, but kept it in its case, tucked away in his closet. From time to time he would take it out, smell its fragrance, and return it to the box. It was a nice gift whose emanations enhanced her memory when they were apart. I am sure he would have kept this handkerchief indefinitely, had not been for a stroke of bad luck.

One of the kids in town, who rode bicycles with us occasionally, stopped by the house one afternoon. He was a thin albino who owned a road bike or *grillo*—cricket—as Cubans called them because of their lean and light frames. His name was Chicho—everyone called him *Chicho the Albino*—and he had a reputation for being foul mouthed, unpredictable, and volatile.

I had had a run-in with him some months before while visiting a tobacco farm in the region of San Luis. Kids were seldom supervised, so we could just roam anywhere we wanted to and explore everything at our leisure. Next to one of the thatched-roof structures where the tobacco leaves were stored so they could dry out of the sun, there was a huge pile—about fifteen feet in height—of the tobacco waste that had accumulated throughout the season. I did not hesitate and started to climb what seemed, from my perspective, a huge mountain. After a few minutes of slipping and sliding on the vegetable debris, I reached the top. That position allowed me to look farther out in every direction; it also gave me a sense of accomplishment because I had been able to reach the highest point.

But I was not alone. Chicho had seen me and now he was climbing the pile as well. I really didn't care; there was room for more than one at the top. What I had not counted on, however, was his unpredictability, for as soon as he reached the spot where I was standing, he started shoving me, trying to make me lose my balance and roll down to the bottom.

"*Chicho, no jodas*," I said, meaning not to mess around, but the more I protested the more aggressive he became, pushing me harder and harder. I did not want to fight, but there came a point when I realized that he would not stop, so the next time he came at me I ducked and hit him hard in the stomach. Momentarily out of breath, he doubled over as he clutched his abdomen. I quickly placed my hands on his shoulders and shoved him forcefully. He rolled down the vegetable mountain, still moaning and gasping for air. He was not hurt, and by the end of the day, when we returned to Pinar del Río, everything had been forgotten.

On that day, when he showed up at the house, Chicho wanted to know if we had a rag with which he could wipe the grease off the chain of his bicycle. I said that I was not sure but that I would ask Teresa. We both went in the house and he stayed in my bedroom while I went to the back of the house to look for the rag he needed.

During my absence, Chicho went into the adjacent room—Ezequiel's—opened his closet, and saw Amanda's handkerchief. Without hesitation or remorse, he took it out of its box and went out to where he had left his bike. By the time I returned from the back of the house, he had already used the perfumed handkerchief to clean the heavy grease off the chain; further, he had run it several times through the sprocket, so the cloth was not only greasy but poked full of holes as well.

He did not seem to think that he had done anything wrong, for when he finished, he had the audacity to fold the ruined handkerchief, put it back in its box and return it to Ezequiel's closet. I told him to leave, that Ezequiel would be looking for him. My words must have sunk in, for he did not show up again afterwards for a long time.

KARMA

Towards the end of that year, my father spoke to Ezequiel's brother and made arrangements for him to come live with us on a permanent basis. It was just as well, since we went to school together and he spent most of his time at our house. The one detail that I did not learn until much later is that my father had petitioned the courts to become Ezequiel's legal guardian, a step short of adoption. Although he could have made that petition instead, he felt that if Ezequiel gave up his last name and adopted ours, it would have been disrespectful to his own father. In reality, nothing had really changed, except that now it was completely legal. Ezequiel continued to attend the services at the Seventh Day Adventist Temple every Friday evening and spent as much time with his brothers and sisters as he had before.

I mentioned earlier that Ezequiel's father had been killed years before by a driver while operating a horse-drawn cart; he must have been very young then, since at that time we had not met yet. A fact that I would find out later was that the lawyer who represented the driver, and got him acquitted, was my father. Perhaps there is an element of karma in this story, since eventually he would become legally responsible for Ezequiel.

The time at Academia Valella had gone quickly; we went to class, did homework, and listened to the episodes on the radio.

We also rode our new bicycles a lot all over town. As the end of the school year approached, we counted the days until our return to the old house in Puerto Esperanza. The prospect of getting away from Pinar del Río for the summer was always an appealing one (Secretly I hoped to resume the clandestine anatomy classes.) That summer, for the first time, Ezequiel would be coming along with us. I can't really say if he had ever seen the ocean but he liked Puerto Esperanza a great deal. We went swimming, fishing, and from time to time took out a row boat on the bay. In other words, nothing out of the ordinary.

Soon after we arrived, Totó stopped in to say hello to Teresa and, as usual, his visits became quite frequent. Although Totó was a very likeable individual, he was not necessarily the most responsible or stable.

Before too long, Ezequiel and Totó were gambling together. This activity went well beyond the bingo games we had just about every night, where the betting amounts were just pennies. (By the way, we used to cheat by leaving the corner numbers in the freezer all day long, thus making them readily identifiable by touch when we put our hands in the bag.)

Nilo Puentes, who was married to our aunt Cándida and also had a house in Puerto Esperanza, decided to take matters into his own hands and cure Ezequiel once and for all of his incipient gambling habit. Nilo was in the tobacco business, always drove a Ford pick-up truck, and was a lot of fun himself.

He showed up one afternoon after lunch and challenged Ezequiel to a game of cards. Ezequiel, of course, did not need any prodding. He accepted right away since he saw the possibility of making some easy money. Nilo was not necessarily any more skilled at playing cards than anybody else; the element that tipped the scales heavily in his favor, compared to Ezequiel, was his unlimited resources.

The game went on for hours; at times it seemed that there would be no clear winner. Towards the end of the afternoon, however, Nilo's financial superiority began to emerge. Yes, he could lose several hands in a row, but with the following one he always doubled the bet, so the mathematical odds were inexorably in his favor. Eventually, Ezequiel's money was gone.

But this was not the end of the game. Completely under the influence of this gambling fever, he brought out his clothes, shoes, and whatever other personal possessions he had and put them up as collateral for a loan. Nilo, of course, gave him the money in exchange for everything he owned. He wanted to teach him a lesson that he would never forget. In less than an hour, using the same strategy, Nilo won everything. Ezequiel was left with nothing except the ragged shorts that he had on. He had even lost the shirt off his back and his tennis shoes. At this point, Nilo decreed that all the clothes and shoes should remain in storage for a month. All the items were removed from the table and placed in the attic.

For the following month, Ezequiel went around shoeless and shirtless, just wearing the shorts that he tied with a piece of rope. No one thought this was either strange or excessive, for he was being taught a valuable lesson. He had brought it upon himself; there was no one else to blame.

Everyone thought that this was the end phase, that he had been cured, and was ready to resume a more normal and sedate lifestyle just doing what boys of that age usually do. We were wrong.

It was almost the end of summer; soon we would be returning to Pinar del Río, to a more structured life with the beginning of the new school year and new academic challenges. One day,

Ezequiel did not show up for lunch. This was most unusual; even though we had absolute freedom to do as we wished, it was tacitly understood that lunch was around twelve thirty. Although we had no watches, we could tell the approximate time by the height of the sun in the sky. We looked for him at the usual places but he was nowhere to be found.

Around six thirty in the evening, just before dinnertime, he showed up. He looked pale, his steps were wobbly and his speech was slurred and incoherent. Immediately we realized that he was drunk. To sober him up, we gave him a cold shower and then put him to bed so he could sleep it off. Later we were to find out that Totó had returned from one of his fishing trips aboard the *bonitero*, had bought a bottle of Bacardí rum, and had shared it with Ezequiel, who had no previous experience with alcohol. The following week we returned to Pinar del Río. (By the way, the anatomy classes never materialized. For reasons unknown, the young woman who worked for Tía Chichí did not return that summer.)

It was decided by my father and Ezequiel's older brother that he needed more structure in order to rein in what was the beginning of a self-destructive pattern. If left unchecked, these tendencies could lead to disastrous consequences. That fall, rather than returning to school with us, he was sent to a boarding school in the province of Santa Clara. This school was chosen because it was owned and operated by the Seventh Day Adventist Church, so he would be receiving not just academic instruction, but moral guidance as well.

Since I was neither consulted nor had any say in the matter, Ezequiel's absence from the house took me by surprise. I just went on with my own schooling and interests. I remember that by then I was spending a lot of time reading; I used my father's easy chair in the *saleta*, because it was comfortable and the place was quiet. Besides reading the classics, like *Don Quijote de la Mancha* and the works of José Martí, I also read—in translation, of course—such novels as *Tom Sawyer* and *The Three Musketeers*. Around that time, I took a subscription to Reader's Digest condensed books which were delivered to the house on a regular basis.

I also began an exploration of the 20-volume set of *El Tesoro de la Juventud*. These books attempted to explain every question that any young person might have, from how movies are made to how the weather is forecast. It also included sections about the different regions of the world and what made them unique. One volume was devoted to very interesting experiments that could be carried out at home with common household items or others that could be easily attainable. I did many of these experiments, but the one that stands out in my mind was a homemade barometer from a mixture of chemicals that I kept in a clear glass bottle.

BACHILLERATO/HIGH SCHOOL

Towards the end of the year I was scheduled to take the entrance examination to the *bachillerato*, or high school. This test was given throughout several days and it measured the students' proficiency in such areas as language, mathematics, and general science. Since the test encompassed such wide and general areas, it was virtually impossible to study for it. It tested knowledge that one either lacked or possessed.

These examinations were conducted at the *Instituto de Pinar del Río* by the faculty of that institution and there were quite a few students who aspired to become part of the incoming class. Rather than being notified individually, the *Instituto* published an alphabetical list of the students who had successfully completed the examination. Finding one's name on the list was, of course, cause for celebration but it also carried with it some unwelcome consequences.

It was customary for the upperclassmen to 'welcome' the incoming freshmen by initiating them into the high school in a way they would always remember and that would last for a while. Once they got a hold of the list, they went out looking for those students, and since the town was not that big, everyone was easily located.

The girls were 'decorated' on their faces and arms with intricate designs, the initials of the perpetrators, or any other markings of their choosing. These markings were done with a very strong solution of iodine, so they could not just simply be washed away; once applied, it was absorbed by the skin and one just had to wait until it faded on its own. The purpose, of course, was to make them look as unattractive as possible.

For the boys the treatment was different but no less effective. Armed with sharp scissors, they efficiently hunted everyone down and cut their hair so unevenly, so close to the scalp, that the only way to remedy this tonsorial butchery was to have one's head shaved.

There was no point in hiding since the names were crossed off the list as the new students were found and officially 'welcomed.' We just wanted to get it over with as quickly as possible, so the hair would have time to grow back by the time the new school year began.

So, every spring after the entrance examinations were conducted and the list published, a new crop of young people could be seen throughout the town, bearing painted faces and shaved heads. I am sure we looked even uglier than I remember.

The only consolation in all this, indirectly, was the certainty that the following year we would be the ones holding the scissors or the flask of iodine as we, too, left our mark on the incoming class. I did ruin a few heads in subsequent years but I have to admit that I did it out of tradition and did not find any satisfaction in this activity.

As a reward for passing the entrance examinations, and to make sure I would not be late for class, my mother bought me a beautiful wristwatch. The case and band were made of rose gold and the dial showed the picture of José Martí, Cuba's greatest patriot. Since it had a special significance, I made sure to keep it in like-new conditions.

With the start of the *bachillerato* came many new challenges and adjustments. While before I only had to go across Independence Park to attend classes at Academia Valella, now my walk was a much longer one since the school was located at the very end of Martí Street. That meant that I had to go through the entire commercial district of town to the *malecón*, a wide boulevard with a median where small trees and flowers had been planted, until reaching the school. That walk, at a brisk pace, took around forty minutes. As I walked down the *calle real*, as Martí Street was commonly called, I usually ran into other students going to the same place. One of those students, by the way, was José Ignacio, the boy who had been with me in the 'anatomy classes' in Puerto Esperanza. Having company made the walk seem shorter than it was. Most of the classes were held in the morning, then we went home for lunch. In the afternoons we came back for the rest of the classes; the last one was physical education. The instructor, Pepito Ruíz, was a big man who had studied and played football in the United States before returning to Cuba and taken that post at the *Instituto de Pinar del Río.* He was strict, but fair, and insisted that everyone be in the best physical shape. To that end, he saw that we engaged in all sports: track, baseball, basketball, as well as a regimen of calisthenics. For those students who were more adventurous, he even offered training—on a voluntary basis—in boxing.

The other classes were the usual academic subjects such as History, Mathematics, Science, English, and Spanish. Of course, I had a foundation in all those subjects, except in English. Even though everyone realized how important this language was to Cuba—after all, the geographical proximity to the United States was an inalterable fact—it was not widely taught in the public schools. Instead, there was a school called *Centro de Inglés* where any student could attend free of charge in the afternoons. They offered five years of instruction, and after the completion of the fifth year, they issued the students a certificate.

My brother Luis and I had also attended the *Centro de Inglés* years before, but only for one day. It was one of those decisions that was made without consulting with us; we were just told that we were officially enrolled and that we would start on a certain date. We did not think about it much, but just accepted it as something else we had to do. After all, we reasoned, it would be great to communicate with *Las Americanitas* in their own language.

Since there was no uniform required at the *Centro de Inglés,* our mother had made white suits for the opening day. I guess that she thought we should look presentable, especially on that first day of classes. What she had not considered, however, was that dressing children in white suits with short pants would be an open invitation to ridicule.

On the appointed day, we bathed, combed our hair, and dressed in our new white suits. The *Centro de Inglés* was about fifteen minutes from the house; by the time we arrived, there was already a crowd of would-be students waiting for the doors to open. All the boys were dressed in regular street clothes and wore long pants. Even before blending into the crowd, we had become the center of attention and it did not take long for the derisive outbursts to begin. We heard anonymous voices, in mocking tone, shouting out such words as *¡Testigo de Jehová! ¡Atalaya!* and other such epithets. (It was customary for Jehovah's witnesses to dress in white.) In retrospect, I realize that there was really no malice behind the comments. Those boys were just following the Cuban tradition called *choteo,* or making fun of anything available, no matter how serious or how trivial.

Luis and I, of course, were rattled by the barrage of comments, so there came a moment when we just said, "*¡Al carajo!*" or, "To hell with it!" and left. Who needed English anyway? I was going to spend the rest of my life in Cuba, so I saw no need to pursue the study of that language. Time, obviously, proved me wrong and just the fact that I am writing this account in English, not Spanish, is the ultimate proof.

Although the academic expectations at the *Instituto* were higher than before, they were by no means unattainable ones. Time just had to be managed more carefully to keep up with the assignments that were handed out on a regular basis. We were treated more or less as adults and were expected to behave as such.

PRESIDENTE/PRESIDENT

J ust as important as the academic component of the *bachillerato* was the social one. As incoming freshmen, we were at the lowest level in the totem pole. We could only look up to the older students who had been admitted before us; they set the patterns of acceptable behavior both in and out of school.

This does not mean, by any stretch of the imagination, that they were in any way trying to be role models for us. Being as young as we were, however, we did not know any better. Logically, if any student should have been exemplary in his deportment, it would have to be the president of the student council. After all, he was the most readily recognizable figure on campus and his actions, directly or indirectly, affected every student on the premises.

His name was Gustavo Pimentel, and the adjectives that come to mind to describe him are erratic, devious, and dangerous. To this day I have no idea how he managed to get elected to a post that carried such responsibility.

Pimentel liked to gamble, and his favorite game was seven and a half—a card game similar to black jack. The only thing he liked better than gambling was winning. Of course, the only way to win most of the time was clear: he had to cheat.

After school hours, usually at the nearby *Trópico Bar*, he would stage his gambling marathons. Eventually, his victims became suspicious of his constant winning streaks and began to grumble, hinting perhaps that there was something dishonest going on. At this point, Pimentel himself would halt the game, and alleging that he wanted everything to be above board and beyond any suspicion, would go, accompanied by his gambling mates, to buy a new deck of cards.

After paying for the cards, he would not even touch the sealed deck, but asked the clerk to give them to one of the other players. They would return to the gambling table, where the cellophane wrapping would be opened and the brand-new deck shuffled for the first time.

Pimentel's winning streak continued uninterrupted.

What was not known was that Pimentel had bought several decks of cards beforehand, taken them home and, after carefully opening the cellophane wrapper, placed the discreet marks that he knew so well. He then returned the cards to the store, without a refund, and asked the complicit clerk to sell him his own cards every time he came to buy a deck. It was a clever and cunning scheme that served him well.

But it was not this habit that had him removed from the important post that he held. Not content with his extracurricular gambling, he decided to extend his pernicious influence to the confines of the *Instituto*.

Taking advantage of his position as Student Council President, he began to call unscheduled meetings of a select group. These meetings were but feeble excuses to stage his gambling sessions within the school building. Eventually, given the excessive frequency of these gatherings, the school authorities discovered his clandestine activities and had him removed from his post.

I already mentioned that I considered Pimentel a potentially dangerous individual. I base my conclusion on a simple fact: he often brought a loaded gun to school. I don't know where he got it, nor did I ever ask him. I know that it was a .22 caliber revolver that he kept hidden in the waistband of his pants. Although he never displayed it at the school proper, he often took it out in the small cafeteria, adjacent to the school, where students usually congregated between classes to have a soda or to eat a snack.

From time to time, he would discharge the gun into the ground, next to the hedges that surrounded the small shop. Everybody scurried out of the way, making sure to create a safe distance. He liked to see people 'dance,' so he provided the music. The logical conclusion of this reckless behavior—a complete disregard for safety—sooner or later had to culminate in a tragedy. It was just a matter of time. Ironically, the victim was not an innocent student at the *Instituto* but Pimentel himself. One afternoon, after performing his usual antics next to the student cafeteria, he returned the pistol to its place inside the waistband of his pants. There was a sudden and unexpected bang, and immediately everyone realized that Pimentel had accidentally shot himself.

He was rushed to the hospital where the doctors, after treating him, determined that his injuries were not life threatening. The bullet had perforated one of his testicles and then had lodged in his inner thigh. As a result, the testicle had to be removed. He returned to school the following week, just as cocky as ever, but I never saw the gun again.

AVIONES/AIRPLANES

One of my classmates, with whom I developed a deep friendship, was Evaldo Cabarrouy. Eventually he would leave Cuba in 1960 and go on to earn a Ph.D. in Economics in Texas and become a faculty member at the University of Puerto Rico, a post that he held until his untimely death in 2002.

Evaldito, as everyone called him, had visited the United States before, liked American music, and was a member of the Boy Scouts. He was also an avid model builder and collector, a hobby that I later acquired because of my association with him. He liked battleships and airplanes, which he displayed on the shelves that were present in his room. I preferred airplanes and as I built the models became quite proficient in identifying the different designations and the conflicts in which they had participated. Of all the models I had built, my favorite by far was the P51 Mustang. Although it was not the fastest plane, I loved the purity of its design and the maneuverability that it had in the air.

In subsequent years Evaldito and I must have built more than a hundred airplane models, complete with their correct insignias and designations. This was one of the ways in which we spent our free time when we were not doing homework. This activity, by the way, was encouraged by our parents since that hobby was both constructive and educational. There came a point that our combined collections were so complete that a three-day exhibit—each model properly displaying an identifying tag with all the pertinent information—was organized at the *Liceo Femenino,* one of the civic organizations in the town of which both Evaldito's mother and mine were active members. We would continue to pursue this hobby for a few short years until we could no longer find the models or the supplies that we needed to complete the projects.

We also spent many hours together trying to master many of the skills necessary to rise in the Boy Scouts and went out camping in different places in the province. Eventually, the pursuit of this activity would become impossible, just like the building of the model planes that we loved so much.

JAZZ

I t was also around that time that I accidentally discovered
jazz. One afternoon, while walking home from the *Instituto,*
I stopped at a record shop that was on the way. Stereo
sound had just been introduced to the market and the store had
a console record player that was being used to demonstrate the
difference between mono and stereo sound.

To that effect, a long playing record was being played on the
new machine. This recording contained simple bits of sound—a
passing train; tires squealing as a driver slammed on the brakes;
a band playing—that lasted anywhere from twenty to thirty
seconds. As I said, it was a record meant to showcase the new
stereo sound.

The mono recording would be played first; the same sound
came through both speakers. Then, the same bit would be
repeated, but in stereo. The sound of the train could be heard
approaching from the left, reaching the center and then fading
away as it exited through the right speaker. The same was true
of the car. It was heard first on the left; then came the sound of
the tires and eventually it dissipated on the right.

Finally, there was music. I had never heard anything like it
before; with the stereo sound, the instruments on the right and
left were individually isolated. I realized immediately that this

was something completely new, that it had not been part of my previous experience, but something that I definitely wanted to explore.

Pinar del Río, needless to say, was not a hotbed of jazz. The only American music that was heard occasionally on the local stations was the new sound of rock and roll, the latest craze from the United States. The seed, however, had been planted. It would not be until years later, while visiting a girlfriend I had while attending high school in the state of Delaware, that I would have the opportunity to develop this interest. Being a jazz fan herself, she had a nice collection to which she added new records on a regular basis. Sometimes we would sit on her couch and make out while listening to The Dave Brubeck Quartet, Miles Davis, or Dizzy Gillespie.

High-school romances, as everyone knows, tend to be ephemeral. At that particular time in my life, being as young as I was, and still trying to deal with the separations from my family, I viewed that relationship as rather permanent. I had focused on her all those feelings of affection which are usually distributed among family, friends and, of course, a girlfriend. She was both an anchor that kept me grounded and a compass that gave my life a sense of direction.

When the inevitable break up came, I was devastated. Once again, I had lost everything. I remember working a lot during that period, just trying to get her out of my mind. Jazz helped me great deal to overcome my heartache.

Later, during my college years in the mountains of West Virginia where only country music could be heard, my record collection sustained me in what I considered to be a cultural desert. Eventually, all the years of exposure to this music, along with fantasizing about being a jazz musician, would be manifested in my novel *Orpheus' Blues*, one of the more satisfying pieces I have ever written.

DESCONTROLADO/OUT OF CONTROL

B esides building model planes and listening to American music, that year I also acquired a Daisy BB rifle. This was not unusual; in fact, since we had guns all over the house and my father had had that long relationship with firearms, it was encouraged that I should also become familiar with them.

Being as young and inexperienced as I was at the time, perhaps I did not fully realize that any weapon, no matter how small or lacking in power, carried with it an underlying responsibility to use it wisely. This rifle, as I stated, was not very powerful and rather easy to use.

Soon I set up a series of targets in the backyard of our house and spent hours practicing and getting to know the capabilities and limitations of that weapon. As time passed, I created more difficult—smaller and more distant—targets but eventually I mastered them all. Empty cans, bottles, and other items were no match for my newly acquired skill.

Next to our house, separated by a wall, was the neighbor's yard. Although the wall, being around ten feet tall, precluded us from looking inside, the higher branches of their beautiful lemon tree were clearly visible. The temptation of those inviting and abundant fruit was too strong to resist, so I made them my next target. But just hitting the lemons, given my sharp aim, was not really a challenge. I decided then to create faces on their surface with the BBs. The two eyes and the nose were kind of easy; the difficult part was the mouth, since it took at least four shots and I wanted it to have a smile. Since the fruits were at different heights and distances in the branches, creating these smiling faces was really a challenge; sometimes, when I miscalculated, rather than a smile I created a smirk, but with every passing day I became more and more proficient.

I would have continued with these 'artistic' creations, but something that I had not foreseen forced me to stop. The cook next door used the fresh lemons to season meat and fish or sometimes to make lemonade. Imagine her surprise upon finding the fruit pockmarked and full of BBs. Since they had no neighbors on the other side (just the alley leading to Africa), she quickly put two and two together and came to the conclusion that the shots were coming from our yard. The lady next door must have complained to my mother because she asked me to stop using the lemons for my target practice.

So there I was, with a rifle full of BBs and no targets worthy of my skill. It was then that I turned my attention to the animals—birds and lizards—that populated the yard. They were moving targets, hence more elusive and challenging but, I now realize, no less defenseless.

Early in the morning, as the temperature became warmer, the lizards would come out to bask in the sun as they rested on the leaves of the abundant flora of the yard. Hidden below, I could discern their silhouettes delineated on the green background. I then took aim and pulled the trigger. The resting silhouette would quickly disappear, lifted off the leaf by the impact of the BB.

Birds were different; they flew into the orange tree that we had and perched on its branches. If they saw movement below they would quickly fly away, so one had to be completely still and with the rifle already cocked and ready. Most of the time I did manage to shoot the birds; they just tumbled down the tree and fell at its base. They lay there for a few minutes, twitching slightly, until the life just went out of them. I even managed once to shoot a hummingbird as it hovered momentarily to suck the nectar from one of the flowers that grew in my mother's garden. I congratulated myself again on my good aim.

This went on throughout the year but the one episode that haunts me, until this day, took place after a long period of rain that caused some of the rivers and creeks to overflow their banks. We were curious about this event, so Luis Mendoza took us out on the road the led to La Coloma, a small seaside town on the southern coast of the province. We stopped several times along the way just to look over bridges and get a firsthand look at the damage that the floods had caused.

Next to one of these bridges, on the side of the road, there was a medium-sized tree. As we got out of the car, what caught my attention immediately was the four small birds perched on one of its branches. They formed a symmetrical line, not unlike those found in shooting galleries. They did not attempt to fly away as we approached the edge of the bridge. In fact, I do not believe that they could fly yet. Maybe they had come out of their nest to dry off now that the rains had subsided.

As insensitive as I was, none of that mattered; I retrieved the BB rifle from the car and, carefully taking aim, shot the first bird. For an instant I thought that the others would fly away, but they didn't. They just stayed perched on the branch, oblivious—or powerless—to prevent what was about to happen. The birds were so close, so still, that they made extremely easy targets.

There was no way I could miss. As usual, I congratulated myself afterwards.

This senseless killing spree went on for a while. Even when we visited Amancio in San Juan y Martínez, I always made sure to take the rifle with me, so I could shoot whatever came within my sight. I was not hunting to ensure my own survival but killing for the sheer pleasure of it. What I did not know, or imagine, was that one random event would soon compel me to shift my perception and make me realize that what I was doing was not just senseless but utterly wrong.

One afternoon, as I returned home from the *Instituto,* I heard the sound of screeching tires as brakes were hastily applied and then the sound of a dog whining in pain. It was a stray dog that had been hit by a car in front of Independence Park, close to our house. The injured animal managed to crawl to the curb, where the sidewalk met the road, and just lay there whining softly and panting. Just by coincidence, the dog had collapsed less than three feet away from me. I did not know what to do; no one else was going to do anything since it was just a stray dog that belonged to no one. Yet, something within me would not allow me to keep walking and ignore the dying animal. I put my books down and squatted next to the dog as I looked into its eyes. He probably knew, at an instinctual level, that he was dying, but he looked at me, perhaps asking me silently to accompany him during his final moments. I reached out and patted his head, attempting to make the transition less difficult. His panting became a subdued breathing, then it stopped altogether. He was gone. To this day I hope that my presence and my reaching out to him made a difference. I kept thinking of that stray dog, that he would never roam the streets again, visit his favorite places, or find pleasure in receiving an unexpected meal provided by a kind but strange hand. Everything he loved was gone in an instant.

From that moment on, I realized how precious, how fragile, and how ephemeral life is. Every living creature clings to it, for it is the only thing anyone really has, even if it is for a short time. That day, I put the rifle away and never aimed it at a living thing again. Since then, I make sure to respect life in all its manifestations. It was a lesson that I learned early in my life, and the price that I paid was a high one, since I will always carry those dreadful images with me.

VENGANZA/REVENGE

As the school year ended, I talked to my father and pleaded on Ezequiel's behalf. He had returned to Pinar del Río for Christmas and at that time had expressed a desire to return. He liked the school in Santa Clara well enough, but he was away from family and friends. I simply asked my father to reconsider his decision; if Ezequiel went off the straight and narrow he could always be sent back. I suppose that my argument was convincing enough since Ezequiel returned and enrolled at the *Instituto* to start classes the following fall.

Unbeknownst to me at the time was the fact that one of my classmates, by the name of Armando, had been bullied on his way to and from school all year long. The other boy, a local tough who did not attend the *Instituto*, would wait for him and beat him up on a regular basis.

I found this rather strange, for Armando was one of the most easygoing guys I knew. He just wanted to go to school and pursue his own interests, just like anyone else. I now realize that some types of behavior cannot be explained rationally since they do not follow any logic at all.

But as easygoing and peace-loving as he was, Armando realized that this situation could not go on indefinitely. In order to put an end to it, he went to see El Águila—The Eagle—a mulatto who trained all the boxers in town. After listening to Armando, El

Águila told him that he only trained the boxers that were under contract, that what he wanted was impossible. Armando was desperate, so he signed a contract that obligated him to have a minimum of three professional fights representing that gym. After this requirement was met, he could retire if he wanted to. He did all this without consulting with his family.

Throughout that summer, under El Águila's skillful direction, he observed a strict regimen of body building exercises and boxing training. Even though Armando's weight could not have exceeded one hundred twenty pounds, El Águila often made him train with boxers that were in much heavier categories. Once, during one of my visits to the gym, I saw him sparing with the heavyweight champion of the province. No wonder El Águila had the best boxers in his stable.

Towards the end of summer, just before the beginning of the new school term, it was time for Armando to take care of the problem that had brought him to the gym to begin with. Accompanied by El Águila, they went looking for the young man that had taken it out on Armando for an entire year. Of course, he was not hard to find and he probably thought that he could repeat the abuse that he had perpetrated with impunity in the past.

El Águila did not say anything but just stepped aside. He knew that his pupil was more than ready; this was just the final test that would corroborate that fact, a ceremony that would give validity to all the hours of training in the gym at the rear of the *Colonia Española*, a social club that provided all sorts of activities.

The local tough threw the first punch, but this time his fist only found empty air. Armando easily and skillfully avoided the blow; it was a move that he had practiced a thousand times before. As he came out of that defensive maneuver, his fist shot out and landed on his opponent's chest. He seemed startled; it was something that he had not expected, but he attributed to good luck and not skill. He charged once again, this time more forcefully, but once again his fists only found empty air.

El Águila had trained Armando well.

It was now time to take the offensive. The attack was both systematic and meticulous; every punch that Armando delivered met its target. I suspect that he intentionally kept from knocking out his opponent; maybe he wanted him to pay him back for all those beatings during the past year.

As the fight progressed, the other boy was visibly becoming more frustrated; after all, he was used to winning and now he could not even connect a single punch. By the end of the session, his eyes, nose and mouth were so bruised, swollen, and bloody that he had become unrecognizable. Armando had, in fact, erased his face. At this point, El Águila stopped the fight. The goal had been accomplished.

But Armando was not in the clear yet. He still had to fulfill his commitment to have at least three professional fights in return for the training he had received. He did not shirk this responsibility and before long his name appeared on the printed flyers that announced the upcoming bouts. These flyers were hand delivered all over town, so he knew that eventually his family would find out that he had to engage in three professional fights. He waited until the day of his first fight to inform his family; they had seen his name on the program but simply thought it was a boxer who shared the same name. At this point, there was nothing they could do about it.

I remember that night vividly; most of the members of our class were present, sitting on the bleachers. When Armando came out, we all stood up and cheered for him. That first fight, in a way, was both a thrill and a disappointment because Armando knocked out his opponent during the first round. When I got home that night, I realized that my throat was hoarse from all the shouting I had done during the fights.

We went to see him fight two more times; he won both bouts and after that third fight, once his commitment had been fulfilled, he retired. Once again, he became a regular student and pursued the sport that he loved the most, which was basketball.

BARLOVENTO

That summer, we were invited by Uncle Joya for a vacation at Barlovento, a suburb of Havana where the houses had been built next to a canal that led to the ocean. One could park the car in front and have the boat in the back. He had just bought that house and loved all its amenities. I was also relatively close to his office and to a small fruit farm that he owned.

Early in the morning, he would wake us up before six by banging a metal spoon on the back of a frying pan. Then we drove to his small farm in Caimito to pick some fresh fruit for breakfast. Afterwards, he would go to his office and return to Barlovento for lunch. We did a lot of swimming and fishing, as well as visiting other places in Havana.

On one occasion, Uncle Joya took me out on his boat; it was a clear day and as we go farther and farther away from the house, the coastline eventually disappeared. The fishing lines, as long as they were, did not manage to reach the bottom of the ocean. We spent the morning out there, just fishing and talking.

When the time to go back arrived, he pulled the rope to start the overboard motor, but rather than hearing the familiar sound, I saw the entire thing engulfed in flames. For a moment I thought we were both going to die, but Uncle Joya simply took an empty can from the bottom of the boat, quickly filled it with ocean water, and poured it over the engine. He did this several times until the fire was extinguished. The motor started without any difficulty and, to my relief, we made it safely back to the house.

Apparently, some of the fuel had spilled and a spark from the motor ignited it, but watching that motor completely engulfed in flames is an experience that I do not want to repeat.

SOLFEO/MUSIC THEORY

That summer would also be the last one we would spend time at the house in Puerto Esperanza, but that would be the least of our problems, not just for us, but for the entire Cuban population.

Throughout this time, my interest in American music, but jazz in particular, had not diminished. Just by chance, a young man by the name of Roberto started courting my cousin Candelaria. He would come to the house every night and they would sit on the *portal* until he left around eleven in the evening. Although he worked at a bank during the day, he was also a trumpet player and held a permanent position in the band of Rolando Lluis, one of the most prominent musicians in the entire province.

Roberto was a really nice guy and I think he was pleased when I showed an interest in music. Being a professional musician, he knew everybody in the business and was fully aware of the opportunities available in the city. He told me that there were music classes, free of charge, available to anyone who was interested. These classes were held at city hall at seven in the evening and the teacher was a member of the municipal band. My parents were all for it, since they always encouraged any type of learning endeavor.

Of course, I did not lose any time; I went down to City Hall and enrolled right away. In my mind I pictured myself with a saxophone in my hands, bringing forth soulful sounds that would inspire sighs of admiration from an imaginary audience.

But reality was quite different. Since the instructor was, as I mentioned before, a member of the municipal band, he was a firm believer that before one could even approach an instrument, a mastery of musical theory was essential. In other words, we had to learn to read music first. This task, if undertaken seriously, was not an impossible one, but in my view a minor setback before I could start really playing.

Every day, after coming back from my classes at the *Instituto*, I would immerse myself in the study of the *solfeo*, as music theory is called in Spanish. I also had the advantage of having a professional musician come to the house every night, so if I had any questions, I would ask Roberto. The subject matter itself did not present any insurmountable hurdles but the classes themselves, and one classmate in particular, made the learning a little more difficult.

The sessions were held—I already mentioned—at seven in the evening in one of the rooms of the City Hall. Although our group was always there a few minutes before seven, the instructor would invariably show up about ten or fifteen minutes late. Our group, by the way, was made up of boys only; most girls who were interested in music studied piano and had private tutors. As time passed, I learned that before coming to class, our instructor liked to stop at a local bar and have a few shots of *Guayabita del Pinar*, that trademark liquor of our province that is distilled from a type of dwarf guava.

The teacher sat at the head of a table and the students came up individually to recite their lessons. If all the quavers, semiquavers, half notes, and rests were not properly observed, that student would have to repeat that lesson. We all noticed, though, that about fifteen or twenty minutes into the session, the teachers' eyes became heavy and he began to doze off under the influence of the *Guayabita*. This did not mean, we soon found out, that we could make mistakes while reciting the lessons. Although half asleep, the teacher's ears were so well tuned that the slightest error would cause his eyes to open immediately and reassign the same lesson for the next class.

Julián, a black kid in our class, was the cause of many lessons having to be repeated. Not that he kept anyone from studying or from approaching the instructor's desk; his tactics were more subtle and insidious.

The windows of the classroom faced an interior courtyard where jasmines, begonias, ferns, and other tropical plants and flowers grew in the flowerbeds. These windows were very tall and with wide doors that reached from floor to ceiling. In order to accommodate them in the room when they were open, they had a long central hinge that allowed them to fold upon themselves. It was behind one of these folded doors that Julián hid while the rest of the students approached the instructor's desk to deliver the assigned lesson. The angle was such that he was hidden from the teacher's view, but easily visible to the students.

At that precise moment, he would unbutton his fly, completely expose himself, and set in motion a silent but explicit phallic ceremony. As if possessed by a priapic demon, he shook his entire body, swayed his hips with lightning speed, and raised his arms with abandon, as if pulsing a set of invisible castanets.

This spectacle was so ludicrous, so intrinsically offensive to the decorum of the classroom and to the dozing instructor, that the logical result was one of uncontrolled laughter. This outburst, without fail, made the student next to the instructor miss some of the notes, thereby causing the teacher to wake up and the lesson to be reassigned for the next meeting.

This happened to me just once, but from that day on I stood in front of the desk, facing the teacher and my back to the class. I knew that if I looked at Julián, I would not be able to contain my laughter and my time studying would be wasted. This ridiculous and unusual event would later surface in my novel *Saga*, in which the main character is forced to take music lessons by his father.

As time went on, I realized that Julián usually did not do very well with his lessons, that he really did not care about learning to read music, and that he was already proficient in several percussion instruments. The only reason that he attended these classes was because his father wanted him to become a member of the municipal band in the future.

I suppose that since he was not making much progress, he wanted everyone else's musical development to remain on a par with his own; these phallic dances were one way of achieving that goal. About a year later, after these classes dissolved, I never saw him again but I often wondered what ever became of him. I would like to think that he is still alive, and playing the African drums that he loved so much.

BOY SCOUTS

My afternoon and evening hours were mostly taken up by my studies at the *Instituto* and the music classes that I have just described. These were the responsibilities that I had to meet, but there was also free time that I used for my personal interests. I kept reading for pleasure, building model airplanes, and listening to American music and even participated occasionally on *Caravana de Hollywood*, a radio show hosted by Reynaldo Montesinos, one my friends from school.

Reynaldo was one of those individuals who discarded his inhibitions—if he ever had any—and did what he wanted, without regard to what other people thought. I suppose that being an extrovert, he would end up with his radio show which made him immensely popular, especially among the girls.

I have already described the rite of making the incoming freshmen shave their heads; no one wanted to repeat that experience. No one, except Reynaldo Montesinos. One Monday morning, he showed up at school with a shaved head, except that at the top he had instructed the barber to create an ace of hearts with hair about a quarter of an inch in length. This odd and daring tonsorial deviation made him even more popular and before the week had ended, other boys donned the ace of clubs, diamonds and spades.

Besides sharing the interest in rock and roll, he also invited me to his show because I would bring to the station records that he did not have in his collection, thus adding variety to the program.

Because of my association with Evaldo Cabarrouy, that year I also joined the Boy Scouts. Our troop was called The Eagles and we had activities most weekends. Of course, we had to learn the Boy Scout manual and pursue knowledge to qualify for the different badges.

As we became more proficient, we were expected to become more independent and participate in the activities that the different troops organized throughout the province. These activities were many, but what I enjoyed the most were those nights when we camped out, sometimes for as long as three days. As it was customary, we carved a notch in our staff for every night we spent camping.

These nights were for the most part uneventful, but one in particular stands out in my mind. After climbing for several hours and crossing a narrow river, we reached *El Cerro de Cabras* (Mountain Goat Ridge) and set up camp in a clearing next to a creek with the clearest and coldest water I had ever seen. The scenery was truly breathtaking because the landscape was so pristine and removed from any traces of civilization and the elevation of the terrain afforded us an unobstructed view of everything below.

As a precaution in case of rain, we made sure to dig some narrow and shallow trenches around the tents; the clearing was not flat, but at a slight incline, and the water would drain downhill. Just in case, I had brought with me an old plastic shower curtain that my mother had given me and it became the floor of my tent, thus isolating me from the bare ground.

After a dinner cooked over an open fire, we cleaned the dishes in the nearby creek and filled our canteens. We had no radio, so to entertain ourselves we told stories and jokes until it was time to go to bed. This, of course, was the whole point of camping, to get away from our daily activities and modern conveniences.

To make sure that everyone was safe, we would take turns keeping guard during the night. My shift was between two and three in the morning, so I managed to sleep a few hours before I was awakened to take my post.

What struck me most about that night was the absolute darkness and the sound of the nocturnal insects whose chirping created an underlying cacophony, a hypnotic background of sorts that permeated the darkness.

As was expected of me, I did not just stay in front of my tent, but walked quietly around the camp, making sure that the entrances to all the tents were closed. In the center of the camp, still smoldering and plainly visible, were the last embers of the fire we had built a few hours earlier. There was nothing out of the ordinary, so I just enjoyed the peaceful night; somehow that locale seemed far removed from everything, completely disconnected from the rest of the world, both in time and distance.

Next to the clearing we had chosen stood a medium-sized tree; I had noticed it when we arrived because of its natural symmetry and harmonious lines. Its perfection almost made it seem artificial. For some inexplicable reason, around two thirty that night, I realized that some fireflies had landed on its branches. I am not an entomologist but I know that the variety of fireflies found in Cuba are much larger than the ones found in the

United States; I would say they are the size of cockroaches. Given this fact, the amount of light they emit is much more profuse and noticeable than their American counterparts. Within minutes, as if summoned by an invisible and irresistible force that compelled them to converge on that spot, the entire tree was covered with fireflies. The first image that popped into my mind was that of a Christmas tree that had randomly been placed on top of that remote ridge. I stood there for a while, just looking at that amazing sight, aware of my good fortune of being at that spot and witnessing something that was not part of most people's experience. Then, as mysteriously and unexpectedly as they had come, they dispersed into the night, leaving behind a deep darkness and that incredible memory that I still carry with me after all these years.

The following morning after breakfast, we left camp to explore the surrounding hills. As we climbed the trails once again, I realized how lucky I was to be a participant of that experience. I was surrounded by friends; everyone was in a good mood and the landscape could not have been more beautiful. What more could I want?

The second night on that ridge was quite different from the first. Right after dinner, some thick clouds gathered, easily eclipsing the setting sun. Somehow, we suspected that the weather would only worsen as the evening progressed and our fears were soon realized.

At first only a few drops fell. Then came a steady rain that by midnight had turned into a relentless deluge. We all took refuge in our respective tents, grateful that we had had the foresight to dig the trenches that channeled the water away from us. As I listened to the rain, I thought of the previous night, of the fireflies and how different things were in just twenty-four hours. Then, when I was almost asleep I felt a stream of water under me. Or rather, water running under the shower curtain that had become the improvised floor of my tent. Although I was still dry, I realized that the force of the rain had overwhelmed the trenches we had dug and exceeded their capacity. There was nothing anyone could do, just wait it out until morning and hope that the rain would stop, or at least abate.

Although I knew that I would not go to sleep, at least I tried to close my eyes and rest. Then I heard someone outside calling my name. I undid the inner straps that held the flaps together and found one of my friends in the rain, asking to come in. He hurriedly came inside and I secured the entrance flaps again. His tent was completely flooded, and since he knew that I had brought along the shower curtain, he wanted to stay where the floor was dry. I said that it was fine—to deny his request would have been an act of cruelty—and that he could stay there until morning.

Once again, I tried to get some rest; the rain kept beating on the sides of the tent and rolling under the plastic underfoot. Within half an hour, three more people came over; I could not turn them away, but by then we could not lie down, but sit up and wait until morning.

By the time the sun rose, the clouds had dissipated and the landscape—at that early hour enveloped in a soft mist—appeared even more pristine than before, cleansed by the torrential rains. Everything was still too wet to build a fire, so we ate some dry food from our knapsacks, took down the tents, and started the trek back to the paved highway that led to the town.

My time with the Boys Scouts taught me a great deal, not only about how important it is to rely on others, but also to try to be prepared for every contingency. No wonder their motto was *Siempre Listo*, or Always Ready. But my dreams of achieving the status of Eagle Scout, along with those of mastering the tenor saxophone and completing my studies at the *Instituto,* would soon be truncated because of circumstances beyond my control.

MOTOCICLETA/MOTORCYCLE

A
t that time, some of the students at the *Instituto*, rather than walking to class or taking the bus, rode motorcycles. The engines had small displacements and would not go extremely fast, but allowed the owners the freedom to move about town as they wished. From time to time, I would catch a ride with one of them and I always found the experience exhilarating.

It did not take me long to reason that the logical step up from my bicycle would be a motorcycle. I had even conceived a plan to get a summer job and save enough money for its purchase. In fact, I had gone down to Abigail's shop on Cuartel and Yagruma and secretly picked out the one that I intended to buy. I felt that this plan would go smoothly; after all, I was now old enough and intended to raise the money by myself.

By that time, I already had a job offer as a helper at a body shop where other young people worked. In retrospect, I should have known from the start that this plan was doomed to fail. One of the prejudices that existed at the time in Cuba, and Latin America in general, was that manual labor was beneath professionals. The son of the most prominent lawyer in the province could not be allowed to work at such an establishment since I would be outside of our social stratum.

I have never looked upon any type of work as demeaning, just so long as it is honest work. This attitude would prove invaluable after my arrival in Miami. While attending high school, and to make some money, I took a job after school in Miami Beach. I was responsible for delivering the newspaper to different sections of a hospital where I also kept several vending machines supplied with the current issue. After taking care of the hospital, I went out on the street to sell the remaining newspapers. At that time, to make that day's paper more current, an afternoon supplement was included. This supplement had a blue line across the top, right above the latest headlines.

I always stood right below a traffic light so I could walk between the cars and sell the papers to the people who were going home for the day. "Blue Stripe; get the Blue Stripe!" I would shout, but back in those days I had no idea what I was saying.

To maximize my profits, I would purposely fumble with the apron where I kept the change. In the meantime, the light would turn green and the driver, exhorted by the impatient honking behind him, would usually tell me to keep the change. It was a nice ploy that netted me some of the extra money that I needed since my parents were not able to help me financially.

As soon as I told my father about my plans to buy a motorcycle, and that I had a job offer at a body shop, I was met with instant opposition on his part. His reasoning was sound: if I ever got into an accident, most likely I would be the one injured or killed. He calmly cited the case of our next-door neighbor (he was a few years older than I was) who had ended up in the hospital.

His mother had bought him a motorcycle to get his approval of her marrying Bigoa, a retired army sergeant. He was a good and safe rider, but one day, as he sped between two rows of cars, somebody opened a door, blocking his path. He had no time to brake; the motorcycle hit the open door and he was catapulted into the air. This accident resulted in a broken arm and other lacerations. After that day, realizing that he could have been killed, he never rode again and shortly thereafter the motorcycle was sold.

Looking back, I realize that my father was right, but being as young as I was the allure of a motorcycle completely clouded the remote possibility of a fatal accident. But he had made his decision, so the motorcycle was out; there was nothing more to discuss. He knew how much it all meant to me, for after making a pause, he said, "If you want to drive something, then drive the family car."

The statement had been so casually made that I could hardly believe it. I was barely fourteen years old, so there was no way I could get a driver's license for another four years. "I will ask Mendoza to teach you," he added. I knew that he was well aware of this fact, but the fact that it did not seem to bother him made me realize, once again, how influential he was.

At that time, I wasn't at all interested in cars. I viewed them as simple utilitarian devices that facilitated transportation. They lacked the mystique and thrills provided by a motorcycle. Besides, my father's car was not a sleek and fast sports car, but the same uninteresting 1952 Ford sedan that we used to go to Puerto Esperanza every summer. Even its dark blue color was kind of boring. But since the motorcycle was out, there was really no alternative except to keep walking, riding the bicycle, or taking the bus.

For the first driving lesson I just sat next to Luis Mendoza while he patiently explained the workings of the car and how to shift gears. The shifter was located on the steering column and there were three forward speeds and reverse. As everyone who drives a manual transmission automobile knows, the most difficult part is mastering the change of gears. Perfect coordination between the left foot, as it releases the clutch, and the right, as it gives gas to the engine is essential. Then, as the car gains speed, one must seamlessly shift into a higher gear, and so on. Luis Mendoza, as experienced a driver as he was, made it all look very easy.

When it was my time to sit behind the wheel, he left the city limits and got on the highway that led to La Coloma, a small coastal town on the southern coast of the province. Once we arrived at a deserted spot on the highway, he pulled over and we exchanged places. Once behind the wheel, and with the engine still running, he had me depress the clutch and go through all the gears. Then, it was time put the car in first and continue on to La Coloma. I tried to emulate the procedure that I had witnessed so many times before, the one that I had practiced mentally, but as soon as I let out the clutch, the engine stalled. Either I had let out the clutch too quickly or had not given the engine enough gas.

Luis Mendoza was not surprised; I imagine that he expected this to happen. "Try it again," he said. "This time give it a little more gas."

I did just as he said and this time the car lurched forward, but did not stall. "Second gear," he said after a few moments, when he heard the engine straining, "And keep your eyes on the road."

He was right; after the car gained speed, it was not that difficult to get to the top gear and keep going. But my training went beyond just steering the car. From time to time, after making sure there were no other cars behind us, Mendoza would make me slow down, thus forcing me to put the car in a lower gear. He just wanted me to sense instinctively what gear was needed at the different speeds. Since this road was usually deserted, on more than one occasion he had to tell me to slow down. He also realized that the power of an eight-cylinder engine, combined with an eager and inexperienced teenager, was a potentially lethal combination. Besides, I was driving without a license, so we adhered strictly to the speed limit just to make sure we had no accidents.

This driving instruction took place several times a week, usually during the late afternoon or early evening when I had finished with my classes at the *Instituto* or the music theory classes at City Hall. As my skill behind the wheel progressed, Mendoza would occasionally allow me to drive back into town and park the car in front of our house.

TOTA

These driving lessons, I now realize, also had an underlying purpose—one a lot more subtle but no less important.

From time to time, on the way back to town, Mendoza would ask me to pull into an ample but unpaved parking lot. Set back from the road, a large structure was the focus of attention; there were no other buildings around. From the very beginning I realized that given its size and construction, this was not a dwelling, but a commercial building.

In the front section there were tables and chairs, and to the left a long counter with about ten or twelve stools. White lattice rising to the ceiling divided the place into two sections. There was no furniture present in the back, just a jukebox with the latest Cuban and Latin American songs.

Mendoza sat comfortably on one of the stools, ordered a beer, and started to chat with a middle-aged woman. It was obvious that they knew each other. Later I learned that her name was Tota, the owner, and that her place did not have a name. It was just known as *El Bar de Tota*, or Tota's Bar.

Of course, I had no idea why we were there. It was clear that Mendoza did not need me for anything, but soon the purpose of the visit became apparent. In the bar, now idle because of the early hour, there were other women much younger than Tota.

"Why don't you dance with one of them?" Mendoza asked.

I was taken aback. First of all, I didn't know how to dance, and I didn't know any of the women there. I was intimidated, almost to the point of being in a panic. I just didn't know what to do. My indecision and inexperience must have been quite evident, for one of the women came over to where I was standing and led me to the back of the rear section of the bar.

The jukebox was already playing, although I can't remember the song; it was probably one of those nostalgic *boleros* that were in vogue in Cuba during the late fifties. She did not ask my name, but from the beginning her actions showed complete familiarity, as if she had known me for years. Guided by the music, I followed her lead as she pressed her entire body against mine. I had never been this close to a woman, especially one older and ostensibly more experienced than I.

When the *bolero* was over, she did not break the tight embrace but waited for the next song to begin and started to move again. By then I had lost all track of time; I was completely immersed in the woman's firm body and the emanations of her perfume. Then Mendoza materialized and I knew it was time to go home.

These random visits to *El Bar de Tota* became an integral part of the driving lessons. The underlying purpose—obviously—was to make sure that I started off on the right track; that is to say, the cultivation of the opposite sex from an early age. After all, how could one become a man without knowing women? It was a concept that permeated Cuban society and one that rested at the very core of popular belief.

I gladly went along with the whole thing, since I viewed it as a golden opportunity that would eventually lead to that first sexual encounter about which every Cuban boy fantasizes with increased frequency. Soon after my first visit to Tota's place I realized that the women who worked there were 'professionals.' Since they were not that busy during the late afternoons, they could indulge the immature teenager who visited the bar with an older man. In time, they hoped, I would become one of their clients. Rumor had it that Tota herself had retired from 'the life' and opened that highly successful enterprise.

The way those women moved, how they touched me and encouraged me to touch them in return was something that would not—could not—happen with girls my age. They would undergo strictly supervised courtships under the watchful eyes of their mothers; such liberties would not be allowed until after the marriage vows were exchanged. According to popular belief, there were just two types of women: those who did, and those who didn't. A middle ground did not exist.

At home, of course, these visits to Tota's Bar were never mentioned, let alone discussed. Now, I am sure that my father was behind it and my mother was completely kept in the dark. It was also part of popular belief that once a boy reached a certain age he should slowly and progressively distance himself from his mother's influence and seek the company of other women, especially if they were older and had more experience. These were the first steps along that road that eventually had to be traveled by every Cuban male.

MACHO/MALE

I had been driving for about six months when Luis decided that he wanted to learn too. Of course, this decision was not mine to make but somehow, he convinced our father that it was the right time. I have no idea how Mendoza felt about the whole thing; he never made any comments but he now had two students instead of one. I do remember that at first Luis had to use a pillow to prop him up on the seat, but that did not last very long.

The driving schedule and itinerary did not change; we went out several afternoons a week, drove to the coastal town of La Coloma and then came back to Pinar del Río. During these trips, of course, we now had to stop more often so Luis could get behind the wheel. Mendoza imparted the lessons with his usual aplomb and within a short time Luis was just as proficient as I was changing gears and maneuvering the Ford on the two-lane road.

Our customary stops at Tota's Bar went on as usual. I assume that Mendoza, after consulting with our father, had come to the conclusion that it was never too early to start off on the right foot. I must confess that at first I had some reservations about Luis, but they turned out to be unfounded. Even though he was younger than I was, Luis always had a magnetism that women found irresistible, a quality he possessed until the day he died. Even as children, when girls came to the house, they always wanted to see Luisito. I never had such luck and to this day I am at a loss to explain the source of that ineffable—and enviable—quality.

From the start, I could tell that Luis felt right at home at Tota's Bar. His light complexion and blue eyes, combined with that self-assuredness that he exuded, even as a boy, made him an instant hit with the women. They loved to dance with him and he took full advantage of those opportunities. He was eager to travel the road that led to manhood and the women there were providing some quick and thorough lessons.

Even though I had visited the bar many more times than he had, I must confess that I never felt quite at home there. Part of me was always on guard, as if something unknown were about to happen at any moment; I just didn't know what. I attribute this to my more reserved, almost introverted personality.

One afternoon, indistinct from the rest, something did happen. As usual, Luis and I were at the back of the bar, dancing with two of the women who worked there; Mendoza was in the front, sitting at the bar and talking to Tota while drinking his beer.

Then, without warning, the woman with whom I was dancing casually lowered her hand and took possession of my private parts. I was so startled that I stepped back, abruptly breaking the tight embrace, and ran out to the front of the bar. It was not a logical reaction, but an instinctive one. Yet, a reaction that was completely out of place. In fact, it was a move that I should have welcomed and enjoyed. After all, we were at Tota's place and the reason for being there was self-evident.

In my state of confusion, I did not get far. A forceful voice, coming from the dance floor, stopped me in my tracks: "¡Carlos, regresa para acá; no seas maricón!" (Carlos, come back here; don't be a faggot!) Yes, it was Luis, reprimanding me for my inexcusable behavior. Above all things, one always had to behave like a man and not like a scared little girl who runs away and hides under her mother's skirt when confronted with an unexpected situation. I went back to the dancefloor and resumed my interrupted dance. Nothing was ever said about this incident, either by my brother Luis or by Mendoza. One thing was certain: that afternoon he had unquestionably proven his supremacy; he was, indeed, a lot more *macho* than I could ever hope to be. There was no way I could ever compete with him; we were, without a doubt, in two different leagues.

TESTOSTERONA/TESTOSTERONE

I have already mentioned that our father was probably behind all this, although his influence was channeled through Mendoza. He certainly knew—and approved—of our visits to Tota's Bar. The only incident in which he had direct participation took a place a short time later.

A special performance by the cast of the Shanghai Theater had been scheduled for a Sunday afternoon at the Riesgo Theater, right across from my father's law firm. At this point I should explain that the Shanghai Theater was located in the Chinese section of Havana and that it had a well-deserved reputation for staging spectacles that went beyond risqué and ventured into the realm of the pornographic. The men who frequented the place were not interested in cultivating their artistic pursuits, but simply in watching the naked women on stage performing their twisted *mise en scenes*. Printed programs, containing provocative pictures, had been distributed throughout the town a few weeks in advance. We could hardly wait!

One afternoon after returning home from school, Luis, Ezequiel, and I were tightly huddled around a small table in my room. We were closely examining the program and anticipating what promised to be an unforgettable performance.

We were so engrossed in that pursuit that we did not hear our father come in. He simply looked down, then took the program from us without saying anything. I am sure we all felt we were in trouble but we could not have been more wrong.

"I hope you are not thinking about going by yourselves," he said. Then after a pause, "I will have to accompany you, just to make sure you are OK." We were thrilled, not just because we were going to the show, but because our intended attendance had changed from a surreptitious escapade to a sanctioned activity.

The next day, I told Evaldo Cabarrouy about it and he asked if he could come with us. Besides building model airplanes and camping with the Boy Scouts, we also shared an interest in women. After all, we were healthy Cuban males; it would have been absurd to expect any less. In fact, from time to time Evaldo and I would to go see European movies that were shown at the Teatro Milanés. Our interest, as one can clearly surmise, was not a cultural one; we were interested in the movies because they often contained partial female nudity.

An incident took place during one of those visits that at the time really shook me. Evaldo and I were at the Milanés one afternoon and I was sitting by the aisle. The movie had already started, so the lights were out. About fifteen minutes later, walking toward me and shaking her ass, came Ayita, a young, thin mulatta who made her living as a prostitute. She often came to that theater in the hopes of picking up prospective clients.

I don't know what possessed me, but as she walked by parading her body, I said out loud, "It's all fake." I thought that she would ignore my idle comment and keep on walking, but I was wrong. She stopped, turned around and stood by my seat. For a moment I feared that she would create a scandal. In my mind I pictured all the lights coming on and everyone staring at me. Of course, the entire episode would be all over town in no time at all. I would bring shame upon the entire family. But that is not what happened. Ayita was not interested in creating a disturbance; she just wanted everyone to know that whatever she had to offer was not fake but the real thing.

"Fake? Fake? Feel that!" she said loudly while shamelessly offering her ass for my inspection. Following that unwritten, yet explicit code to which Cubans adhered, I did as she commanded, but I was in for another surprise. As I reached out, not only did my hand find Ayitas's firm flesh, but many other anonymous and hungry hands that belonged to the men who were sitting nearby. They, too, were eager and ready to take full advantage of the unexpected opportunity that had materialized.

This type of incident shows a clear perspective of our frame of mind before that memorable performance by the cast of the Shanghai Theater. All that testosterone that was now present in our systems had placed our libidos in a state of overdrive.

On the appointed day, the four of us walked down to my father's office where we were to meet Evaldo. Although still early, he was waiting for us. Across the street, even though the ticket booth had not yet opened, a crowd of men had already gathered. A few minutes before one, we crossed the street and joined the throng. The show was scheduled to start in just a few minutes but the ticket booth mysteriously remained closed. At first I thought nothing of it; maybe the performers had been somehow delayed.

After twenty minutes of waiting, the crowd became visibly restless. Some knocked on the glass enclosure of the ticket booth; others began to bang on the doors of the theater. A tall black man, standing on the steps that led to the front door, made a plea for more patience: "*Calma lobos, que hay dulce para todos.*" (Settle down wolves, there is enough candy to go around.) His plea fell on deaf ears. By then the crowd had turned into an angry mob that demanded that the show should commence at once.

What followed was not only unexpected, but in a way ironical. About twelve or fifteen policemen, clubs in hand, materialized and told everyone to go home; there would be no show. At once there was a unanimous uproar of dismay mixed with anger. Everyone had been looking forward to the performance for almost a month; to cancel the show at the very last moment went beyond cruel; it was an infamy. Of course, the policemen were not there to debate with the crowd; those who resisted were encouraged to clear the premises with the tip of their clubs.

Later that day, we found out that a commission from the Women's League for Decency had put pressure on the local police to cancel a show that was a blatant affront to public morals and one that especially portrayed women as mere sexual objects. It was The League's duty—the women felt—to protect their husbands and young sons from such depraved spectacles.

In retrospect, I realize that they were correct but at the time I was just as disappointed as all those hungry wolves that the police had to disperse with their batons. In view of those developments and realizing how disappointed we were, our father treated us to ice cream at the Hotel Ricardo which was on the same block as the Riesgo Theater. He was rather philosophical about the whole thing; I suspect that he knew all along that many other opportunities would come along in the future.

HUELGA/STRIKE

A round that time, and as a direct result of an attempt on president Batista's life the previous year, the repressive measures of the government intensified. Everyone in the country knew that we were living under a military dictatorship; in 1952 Batista had staged a coup d'état to depose Carlos Prío, the previous constitutionally elected president. Elections were held shortly afterwards and he had remained in power ever since, but opposition to his regime was growing.

Being as young as we were, there was nothing we could do about the political situation. We tried to maintain as normal a life as possible; we went to school, socialized with friends, continued with the Boy Scouts, and I kept up with my music classes. But ultimately, that was not enough. As a reaction to Batista's harsh policies, a series of spontaneous strikes were staged by students throughout the nation.

El Instituto de Pinar del Río was not exempt. One morning, during the short time we had between classes, the head of the student council stood on the steps of the stairway that led to the second floor, and citing the brutalities of the Batista regime, called for a general strike. Right away another group of students—apparently in previous concert—went out to the street in front of the school and set some old tires on fire as they chanted slogans demanding Batista's resignation. No one was in class; everyone had gathered around the burning tires, if not out of political conviction, at least propelled by youthful curiosity.

The police arrived within minutes. Since they could not force the student body to return to class, their immediate job was to disperse the crowd and put out the burning tires. Just as they had done during that Sunday at the Riesgo Theater, they took out their clubs and went to work. I did not stick around to ascertain the efficacy of their tactics; I ran as fast as I could and eventually found myself in a narrow street parallel to the back of the school. From the distance I could see the open field where the sporting events were held and the dark smoke rising into the blue sky. The crowd had been dispersed, but the school remained closed indefinitely.

Given this unforeseen situation, which was completely beyond my control, I tried to keep up with the subjects I was taking by reading the textbooks. It was not quite the same as having the teachers there, especially with math and sciences. I also read more for pleasure and my interest in music intensified.

To pass the time, we also made our own version of Monopoly. It took a while to cut out the cards, color them to match the board, and write the rules in Spanish, some of which we made up as we went along. By the time we finished, we had a working version of the game. The main difference was that rather than buying Marvin Gardens and similar properties we were now trying to acquire Tota's Bar and other familiar places in town. So successful was this game that one of our friends, who worked at a pharmacy that often stayed open throughout the night, borrowed it and never gave it back. Apparently, they played while everyone else in town was asleep; it was a way of staying awake just in case a customer showed up.

PASODOBLE

During the afternoons we continued going to La Coloma to sharpen our driving skills. By then Ezequiel had returned from the school in Santa Clara and often came along with us. One of those afternoons, Luis was at the wheel and on the way back to town we had to pass a house where a police car was usually parked; this was not out of the ordinary, since we had seen the car there many times before. This patrol car had been assigned to lieutenant Castañé, a well-known figure in town. It was also a known fact that he took special pride in keeping his patrol car in immaculate condition.

Since we were already on the outskirts of town, Luis was not driving very fast but somehow, he miscalculated and the right corner of his front bumper hit the rear one of Lt. Castañé's patrol car. There was no damage to either car but the impact of metal hitting metal made a very loud noise.

We pulled over in front of his house just to make sure that nothing had happened to either car. Within a minute, alerted by the loud noise, Castañé appeared at the front door wearing his full uniform.

"What is going on here?" he demanded, exhibiting that air of arrogance usually found in those used to being in a position of authority. By then Mendoza had stepped out of the car. He was not excited; his voice did not change from its usual calm tone.

"Nothing happened," he offered. "You can see for yourself that no damage was done."

"And why are minors driving on city streets?" he went on, ignoring Mendoza's words. "That is clearly against the law."

"It's nothing," insisted Mendoza. "Besides, these are Luis Alberto's kids."

Once again, I had tangible proof of my father's influence in the town. As soon as he heard the name, Lt. Castañé knew that it would be pointless to pursue the matter since my father now occupied the high ranking post of magistrate of the supreme court.

"I don't care if they are Jesus' children," he said, still incensed, "and I don't give a damn if they want to kill themselves. Just do it away from my house."

At this point, he was just venting his anger and his frustration that he would not be able to do anything about the whole thing. We just got back in the car—Mendoza was behind the wheel—and drove away.

I thought this would be the last time I would ever see Lt. Castañé but I was wrong. On December 31st, 1958, my parents had decided to go to the Rumayor Club, one of the more exclusive in Pinar del Río, to welcome the new year.

Despite the deteriorating political situation, no one expected anything radical to happen. The focus of the rebellion was in Oriente province, the easternmost of the island. Pinar del Río was at the other end, so everyday life, except for the occasional strikes, had not been disturbed that much. Besides, under the auspices of Batista, elections had been held and the new presidential candidate was scheduled to be inaugurated after the arrival of the new year.

The five of us were sitting at a table, eating and drinking, when

Lt. Castañé appeared and approached us. After greeting my parents, he looked at the three of us. He was visibly in a jovial mood; maybe he had been drinking. Then, looking directly at Ezequiel he said, "You are the one who hit my car and tonight I am going to settle that account." We, of course, did not know what he meant but Luis was laughing since he had been the one behind the wheel on that particular afternoon.

"As punishment," Lt. Castañé went on, "I want you to dance a *pasodoble* for me," he said as he pointed to a woman in a tight red dress. Everyone knew that she was his mistress and one of the best looking women in town.

Ezequiel had no choice; by then the woman was next to him and the band was playing. He made the best of it and followed her lead on the dance floor; everybody was having a good time. The three of us, by the way, had a special reason to look forward to the new year. Luis Mendoza had hinted that we should start off the year in the right way, that we were ready. Although he did not say it in so many words, we knew that somehow a rendezvous with 'professionals' had been scheduled, and that in a few short hours we would cross that threshold that separated men from boys.

Little did we know that our world, with all the rules and traditions that reached beyond the founding of the Cuban Republic, would soon be replaced by an unimaginable scourge; it would plunge the entire nation into the darkest chapter of its history, strip every citizen of his constitutional rights, and disperse much of the population to every corner of the world. In short, everything, as we knew it, was about to end.

EUFORIA/EUPHORIA

New Year's Day, 1959, Cubans woke up to a mood of chaotic jubilation. Batista had fled; the dictatorship was over. There was a bright future ahead. Everyone in the nation assumed that elections would be held within a short time and that the rights afforded every citizen under the 1940 constitution would be immediately restored.

I distinctly remember waking up to the anti-Batista shouts of the crowd that had gathered at Independence Park. Within that unbridled and euphoric mood, one fact clearly stood out: the dictator was gone.

What many people did not realize at the time, perhaps momentarily blinded by the joy of the immediate reality, was that a power vacuum had been violently created. Somehow, it had to be filled.

The chaos during those first few days was absolute; no one was in charge. Of course, the local police were completely ineffective and Batista's army had been rendered useless.

Needless to say, the special plans that we had for that day—so carefully structured by Mendoza—were cancelled. There would be plenty of other opportunities.

It was during that first week that Fidel Castro, taking full advantage of the general confusion that pervaded the nation, boisterously announced a victory march that would begin in the mountains of Oriente province and culminate in his revolutionary group taking charge of the government when they arrived in Havana. Although they were not the only group that had opposed the Batista dictatorship, from the start they claimed to be victors in the struggle, thus relegating every other opposition group to the background.

This historic march, to further support their claim of victory, was broadcast on national television. In every town there were stops for celebratory gatherings. A week later, the march ended at the José Martí Plaza in Havana. A long-winded speech—full of rhetoric, utopian promises and white doves—culminated the event. Free elections were supposed to take place within eighteen months. Cubans thought, now that Batista had fled, that their problems were over.

PAREDÓN/FIRING SQUAD

The year 1959 could accurately be described as a national blood bath. Anyone in any way associated with the Batista regime was rounded up and jailed indefinitely—a clear violation of the 1940 constitution. Many civilians were tried by military tribunals and swiftly executed by firing squads. Free elections were no longer mentioned. Capital punishment had never existed since the inception of the Cuban Republic in 1902. Those in power seemed eager to make up for lost time since the firing squads now worked around the clock and the executions were broadcast live on national television. Years later, and based on these atrocities, I would publish a short story entitled *Cuba: 4 A.M.* while attending Concord College in Athens, West Virginia.

The new regime, drunk with power and without opposition—those who dared to protest the abuses of power and violations of human rights were quickly labeled 'antirevolutionary' and immediately silenced or jailed—began its rampant roster of reforms aimed at overhauling the very foundation of Cuban society.

The first step was to seize control of the media. Newspapers, magazines, radio, and television stations were confiscated in the name of the Glorious Revolution. Once in possession of all news outlets, the new government was able to control, suppress, or modify the news that would be disseminated to the population. Even during the harshest dictatorships in Cuban history, when censorship had been imposed, the news media had remained in private hands.

To spread their message even further, loudspeakers were installed on telephone poles throughout the town; propaganda was now constantly being force-fed to the citizens from morning to night even as they walked the streets.

Education was next. All schools in the nation now fell under the direct control of the government. Teachers had to sign statements of allegiance and adhere to a modified curriculum that oftentimes was nothing more than thinly veiled propaganda. Both teachers and students were exhorted to join the government-sponsored 'voluntary' work brigades. While before Cuban schools were places for the free exchange of ideas, they were slowly turning into intransigent institutions where independent thinking was considered suspicious behavior, and the open embrace of communist dogma was not only encouraged but rewarded.

Despite this chaotic and unstable environment, we tried to maintain as normal a life as possible. We went to school, came home, did homework, and socialized with friends. But one incident early that year made me realize that everything was not as usual, that everything I thought stable and immovable—the very precepts on which Cubans based their lives—were beginning to shift and crumble.

VIOLACIÓN/VIOLATION

One afternoon, without warning, a small group of soldiers knocked on the door and curtly announced that they had come to search our house. Even though they lacked probable cause and a search warrant, there was no point in opposing them. Since they would be searching the house separately, my mother quickly told us to accompany them, just to make sure they did not plant anything that later could be used against the family.

I followed one of the soldiers quietly, watching everything he did. When we came into my room he asked me to open my closet. I did as he requested, then stepped aside. He looked inside, carefully inspecting the contents and looking for something out of the ordinary. Unexpectedly, his attention shifted to the left corner. This was the spot where I kept the Daisy BB rifle. He brought it out, but then realized that it was not a real weapon, so he put it back without saying anything. Yet, he was not completely satisfied. At the bottom of the closet where I kept my shoes, he found the canteen that was part of my camping equipment. He inquired and I told him that I was in the Boy Scouts. He seemed to believe me, for he also put it back and closed the closet door. By then the other soldiers had returned from other sections of the house. They left as abruptly as they had come. No apology for the blatant intrusion was ever offered.

These visits would become routine, so from that point on we were always ready not to have in our possession anything that could be misconstrued as evidence of opposition to the new regime.

Shortly thereafter, a group of men showed up at the house. They were dressed in civilian clothes; they had not come to search the house one more time, but in their possession they had a document giving them the authority to take our family car. This was the same 1952 Ford that my father had owned for years and that he had paid off in monthly installments. A blatant abuse of power, but at this point there was nothing anyone could do. The government could simply claim that any personal property—usually belonging to those known to oppose the regime—had been acquired with ill-gotten funds and that they were simply reclaiming it in the name of the People's Revolution. This was just one more clever ploy to further entrench themselves in a position of power and place their potential adversaries—whether real or imagined—at a clear disadvantage. Citizens all over Cuba were being subjected to this type of treatment. Since my father owned no land or any other tangible assets, the car was the only item they could take from him.

When this happened, I do not recall my father showing any emotion at all. Perhaps he knew that at this point it was useless to oppose those in power, especially over an old car. My feelings, on the other hand, were quite the opposite. The car belonged to the family; it had taken years to pay it off, and I had some very fond memories of the hours I had spent behind the wheel.

From time to time in subsequent months, I would spot the car somewhere in town with a stranger driving it. I felt an inner rage that was manifested in a string of mental curses and profanities directed at the stranger who now had the use of the vehicle. These personal abuses and violations, as well as many others, would be described decades later in my novel *Forgotten Objects*.

PRISIÓN/PRISON

One morning, indistinct from the rest, my father was not there. The soldiers had come in the middle of the night and taken him away. No formal charges had been filed against him, but this was not unusual. The new regime had the power to detain citizens indefinitely, release them at will, or put them in front of a firing squad. It was then that I realized that my father's former influence had vanished. We were now dealing with a government that had a complete disregard for the rule of law.

Later we were to find out that he was being held at the local prison, like a common criminal, and that soon he would be tried for 'crimes against the revolution,' a phrase so vague that it could mean anything.

Right away we got in touch with Luis Mendoza, who in turn alerted my father's closest friends. Since no formal charges had been made, and no appearance before a judge had been scheduled, the idea of being released on bail until the day of the trial was an absurd one. As I said, we were in a situation where law and order had completely broken down, to be replaced by the whimsical and mercurial designs of people who had no regard for constitutional rights or due process.

After doing all that we could and getting in touch with anyone who could remotely be of help, there was nothing left to do but wait. Eventually, a date for the trial would be placed on the docket but until that time, the specific charges against my father would not be disclosed. In my mind, as the naïve teenager I was at the time, none of this made sense. Everybody knew that, according to Cuban law, one either had to be formally charged or released within seventy-two hours after the arrest. I felt that he *had* to be released at any moment; it was the fair and lawful thing to do.

My father, on the other hand, from the perspective of his prison cell, knew better. He realized from the beginning that all semblance of lawfulness and fair play—the very cornerstones of Cuban law—were being quickly and inexorably eroded with each passing day. His stay at the local prison, for all he knew, could be an indefinite one.

Prison food, no matter where one lives, has earned a well-deserved reputation for being of the lowest quality. Cuba is no exception. Since that unfortunate incident that caused him to temporarily lose his vision, my father had been following a low-fat diet, one that certainly the prison was not about to accommodate. Several times a day we accompanied Luis Mendoza to the prison to bring the food that my mother had cooked for him. We always waited for Mendoza in the car while he went inside; my father had left strict instructions that he did not want his children to see him behind bars.

It was during his stay in prison that, unbeknownst to me, my father wrote his last will and testament. This document, besides being a list of possessions that he would bequeath his heirs, was also a recounting of his life and the circumstances that had led to his imprisonment and the unjust charges that he faced. It would not be until years later, when this document reached my hands, that I fully realized how difficult those days must have been for him. He spoke of "...life in prison, where so many indignities must be endured, where so many friends turn their backs, where so many disappointments become reality." He also spoke of "...the long and painful days that never end, of the seemingly endless and sleepless nights when one thinks that dawn will never come."

Within that framework of daily uncertainty, we still tried to continue with our studies and maintain as normal a life as possible. It was what our father wanted, so it was the least that we could do. Needless to say, by this time the Boy Scouts had dissolved and the music classes had been discontinued.

One day, we learned that the date of the trial had been placed on the docket. It would be held at the Palace of Justice in Pinar del Río, a building I had visited many times before to accompany my father and watch him defend his clients. This upcoming trial, without a doubt, would be the most important of his judicial career since he would be defending himself. We also learned that he was to be tried by a civil court and not a military one. This detail may seem trivial, but in reality, it was very good news. The new regime often tried civilians in military courts—a contradiction in terms if there was ever one—where the guilty verdicts had already been decided beforehand. These 'trials' were nothing but *pro forma* exercises, a sham that served as a preamble for the death penalty in front of a firing squad.

My father, despite his precarious situation and his advanced age, had not been idle. While in prison he had been carefully preparing his defense. Another piece of good news was that, as of yet, the 1940 Constitution had not been repealed. Supposedly, despite the constant violations by the new regime, it was still the law of the land.

On the day of the trial, we were all present at the Palace of Justice. My father did not appear any different than I remembered him—he wore a gray suit, white shirt and his customary bow tie—but now I am sure that he was not the same man that had been taken away in the middle of the night months before. His demeanor was one of complete confidence; after all, it was generally agreed that he was the best lawyer in the province. Knowledge of the Law was his undisputed domain and he was prepared to showcase his expertise one more time.

After the charges against him were read, "Conspiring Against the Powers of the State," the witnesses were called to testify. These were rather vague charges, mostly based on his previous association with the Batista regime, and from the beginning it was obvious that they did not have any tangible evidence against him. Since he was representing himself, my father had not only the opportunity, but the right to cross-examine every witness.

The defense, of course, had its own witnesses but the one that surprised everyone and who had a great influence on the outcome of the trial was Joaquín Fernández de Armas. Joaquín had been a member of the communist party for many years and he now occupied a prestigious position in the new regime. He was also a lawyer who had done his apprenticeship at my father's law firm, so he had known him for a long time and knew what kind of man he was.

When his time to testify came, he brought to light that although my father had held an important post during the early years of the Batista regime, he had also resigned from that post and publicly denounced the regime as corrupt. How could anyone who had so openly repudiated that administration, he asked rhetorically, be accused of being one of its sympathizers?

On the last day of the trial, when both the prosecution and the defense were to present their summations, was when my father showcased his expertise as a lawyer. Not only did he address all the vague and unsubstantiated accusations with which he had been charged by the present government, but he also used this opportunity to carefully cite all the constitutional violations that had taken place since his arrest and incarceration. In short, his summation was not just a defense of his own case but a clear indictment of a government that, according to constitutional law, had usurped power. The constitution was clear and still in force, so he demanded that everyone should adhere to these guidelines.

The deliberation did not take very long. All the charges were withdrawn and, as of that moment, he was free to go. There was no rebuttal to the charges that my father had made against the government, nor was there any sort of apology offered for the unjust treatment that he had received.

The news of his acquittal was broadcast on the radio and covered by the local papers. The main thing, as far as we were concerned, was that now he could come home and go about his business. At that time, I still looked upon him as indestructible and not as the seventy-four-year-old man that he really was.

TARZÁN/TARZAN

D espite the constant state of turmoil and uncertainty that was now an integral part of daily life, we continued attending the *Instituto*. After all, that is what we were supposed to do at our age. It was also natural to seek the company of people our own age.

It was around that time that I met Enrique. Being two years older than I was, he had already finished his secondary studies and worked at a local jewelry store. He was tall, lean, and very muscular, so everyone called him Tarzán. We became friends instantly because we shared a like for American music and a dislike for what was going on in Cuba at the time.

Enrique was also an Elvis Presley fan, so I invited him to my house to see my Elvis collection. This was the time before Elvis went into the army, so he had not released that many records yet, but somehow I had them all. He was truly amazed that I had all his LPs and I let him take some of them home so he could listen to the music at his own leisure.

Since the music classes had been canceled and the Boy Scouts had been dissolved, Enrique and I saw each other several times a week. I did my homework in the afternoons, so my evenings were pretty much open. We did not go to any place regularly but just walked around the town in search of anything interesting.

One particular incident, which took place that December,

stands out in my mind. This is the month in which the feast of Saint Barbara is celebrated, but this saint, as every Cuban knows, has been syncretized with Shangó, one of the more powerful and popular deities of the Yoruba pantheon. On this date there would be gatherings of believers; the effigy of the saint would be present, candles would be lit, and offerings placed at the foot of the altar.

By then I had already witnessed the *bembé* that I described earlier, so I knew that *Santería* was quite a serious matter in Cuba. Although not a follower myself, I always respected other people's beliefs. Enrique, on the other hand, was a lot more casual about religious matters, so I was surprised when he invited me to accompany him to a house where they were celebrating the feast of Saint Barbara. But I readily agreed and about nine o'clock that evening we showed up at the appointed place. I had never been to that house, nor did I know anyone in attendance. The living room was full of people and the lights had been turned down. The focus of the room was the corner altar where the effigy of the saint, surrounded by votive candles whose light was reflected on the sword that she held, commanded the entire enclosure. From time to time, someone would approach the corner of the room to make an offering consisting of a box of cigars or a bottle or rum.

We mingled with the people there for a while, just conversing and listening to the percussion music that augured the beginning of the celebration. There was really nothing out of the ordinary going on. I kept asking myself why we had come, but that question would not be answered until we left the house.

Enrique kept talking to the people in the room, but as he did so, he also kept getting closer to the altar. This did not seem significant at the time since people were moving around the room all the time. A short while later, he came back to where I was standing and said that it was time for us to leave. In a way I was glad since I felt out of place in the company of that crowd of strangers whose beliefs I did not share.

Once we were about a block away from the house, he opened his shirt and produced a bottle of Bacardi rum that he had swiped from the altar.

"We can drink it at the river tomorrow," he said. "Isabelita and one of her friends will join us." Somehow, I was not surprised.

Isabelita was a young woman that I had met casually one night during one of our outings. She seemed to know Enrique, for as we walked by her house she called out his name from within. We stopped and she came out to say hello. This in itself was not unusual, but the fact that she was wearing just a skirt and a thin, translucent negligee was. We talked for a while and then she went back inside, apparently not aware, or concerned, that the upper part of her body was plainly visible under the light cast by the street lamps.

We had met Isabelita many other times before, but now, for the first time, I would be alone with her in a secluded spot by the riverbank; Enrique would surely be going off with the other girl. I was understandably nervous but Enrique assured me that there was nothing to worry about. Isabelita was, as he described her, "A sure thing." We were friends, so he was looking out for me.

The following afternoon, around two o'clock, I met Enrique at his house and then we walked over to Isabelita's place which was on the way to the river. He had the bottle of rum from the night before and some cups; in all respects it was supposed to be a memorable afternoon. The girls were waiting for us and seemed to be as enthusiastic as we were about the prospects for the afternoon. I had never met Aida, Isabelita's friend, but apparently she and Enrique were acquainted, for they paired up right away.

Since Enrique led the way, we had no difficulty in finding the secluded spot that he had mentioned before. It was a small clearing by the water, nestled under the tall fronds of surrounding trees and sheltered from view by the thick growth of fluvial vegetation. It was, indeed, a perfect place for a clandestine assignation with a woman.

We sat on the protruding roots of a tree and Enrique served the drinks. We drank, made small talk, and joked for an indeterminate amount of time; then Enrique, after replenishing my cup and Isabelita's, stood up and took Aida by the hand. They disappeared out of view with the rest of the rum and their own cups.

I was alone with Isabelita.

At once the atmosphere became tense. I realized that it had been Enrique, with his jokes and casual demeanor, who had kept the buoyant mood going. I tried to maintain the same tone, but with every passing minute I realized that I was failing miserably. In desperation I took another sip of my drink, hoping to find the necessary courage to do what needed to be done. After all, as Enrique has assured me, it was "a sure thing." At that moment, I knew that Isabelita wanted me to sit closer to her, put my arm around her shoulders and kiss her as I whispered romantic things in her ear. Afterwards we would see where everything led us. My brain kept telling my body to act but somehow I could not find it within me. I was a failure.

I started babbling about my courses at school, the books I was reading, and anything else that came into my head. Nothing had anything to do with the present situation; this was not a time to talk, but to act as a Cuban male. I don't know how long we stayed in that secluded spot but I do know that she was thoroughly disappointed.

After a while, Enrique and Aida reappeared. By the disheveled appearance of their clothes I knew that they had not been talking much; the rest of the rum was gone. Since it was getting late, we started back to town and dropped off the girls at Isabelita's house.

Afterwards, I told Enrique what had happened—or rather, what hadn't happened—but, as usual, he did not seem concerned. "You'll make it the next time," he said casually. "Don't worry about it."

That next time, however, never came. A few weeks later I realized how lucky I had been that afternoon. While talking to a friend from the *Instituto*, I mentioned casually that I had gone out with Isabelita. He looked at me and then told me the story of how Gustavo Pimentel had forced her, at gunpoint, to perform fellatio on him. Although I had no way to corroborate this fact, after that day, just the thought of kissing her became a most unappealing one.

ARTISTA/ARTIST

I t was also through Enrique that I met Dionisio René Barrera, a local artist. His studio was located in an old and dilapidated building, but as a struggling artist, it was all he could afford. There were easels and canvasses everywhere; an old table held containers with brushes of different thickness, tubes of pigment, and a palette.

Dionisio shared with Enrique and me a love for American music, especially the songs of Elvis Presley. In fact, he looked like Elvis: he was tall, slim, had jet-black hair, and long sideburns.

That first day we did not talk much about art (a topic about which I was completely ignorant at that time), but about our favorite American songs and performers. I already mentioned that I shared my record collection with Enrique, so on that occasion I extended the same invitation to Dionisio, which he accepted gladly.

After that day, as our friendship grew, my visits to the studio became routine. With time, I learned that Dionisio came from a very humble family and that he had graduated from *La Escuela de Artes Plásticas* in Pinar del Río. This accomplishment had been achieved through great sacrifices—scholarships and help from friends and family—since he had absolutely no money. I suspect that the reason he was so slender was because he often went without eating in order to pay the rent at the studio or to defray the expense of his art supplies. One thing, however, was undeniable: he had a great artistic talent.

Besides art, Dionisio had one other love: Yolanda. She was a local dancer and perhaps one of the most beautiful women I have ever met. Her cinnamon complexion was complemented by long, straight hair and very fine features. But it went beyond her looks. Her movements were fluid, almost feline. Once I saw one of her performances at the Riesgo Theater and immediately understood why Dionisio was so taken with her. The movements of her supple body awakened something primeval that we all carried buried deep within us, something that momentarily overwhelmed the thin patina of civilization and made us retrogress to a more basic, instinctual level where logic and reason were mere obstacles in the way of pure passion.

Although I never had a conversation with Yolanda, I was very much aware of her presence whenever she was around and I secretly envied Dionisio for having a relationship with her. The thought of making a pass at her never occurred to me; after all, she was Dionisio's girlfriend and I am sure she would not have taken me very seriously since I was younger than she was. Years later Yolanda and Dionisio were married, but by then I had already left Cuba.

Cognizant that Dionisio needed work, I introduced him to my family. My mother was so impressed by his talent that she commissioned a portrait of herself. I still remember Dionisio coming to our house and my mother posing in the dining room. That portrait turned out very well and it hung in our house for many years afterwards.

My mother had always fancied herself a patron of the arts; our house had always been a focal point of poets and musicians. In concert with Tía Panchita, she took it upon herself to make Dionisio's name a household word. Using their life-long connections with the *Liceo Femenino*, they organized a one-man exhibition of Dionisio's work. Programs were printed and flyers were distributed throughout the town. This was a massive project since all the different canvasses had to be moved and placed strategically, and many were still without frames.

That show was a complete success and it led to other opportunities and increased work for Dionisio. Eventually, he would inevitably leave for Havana in search of wider horizons. But it was also inevitable that the ever-increasing demands of allegiance by the communist government would force him to seek his destiny elsewhere.

One day, after our departure from Cuba to the United States, Luis and I received a letter from Tía Panchita. Dionisio, she explained, had the opportunity to immigrate to Venezuela but the airplane ticket had to be purchased in American dollars, a currency that was unavailable to the residents of the island. At that time Luis and I were working at a mental hospital in the state of Delaware, and even though we were not making much money, we saved the required amount and sent it to Tía Panchita. Within a short time, Dionisio managed to move to Caracas where he continued with his art work. Besides exhibiting and selling his work, he also became an instructor in one of the more prestigious plastic arts schools in that city. Throughout his artistic career he also visited the most famous European museums, including the Louvre, in order to study firsthand the works of the masters that he knew so well.

One would think that this is the end of a very successful story, but unfortunately it is not so. Ironically, the same restrictive and intrusive government that Dionisio though he had escaped materialized in Venezuela under the rule of Hugo Chávez and later Nicolás Maduro. As I write these lines, Dionisio is once again trying to escape the stifling environment and make his way to the United States, where his son lives. I have been in touch with both of them and, once again, have tried to help expedite matters with a monetary contribution towards that end. Much of his work is now in the United States, and it is my hope that he will arrive soon so he can resume his artistic career in a more favorable environment.

NUNCA MÁS/NEVER MORE

It is only natural for men, especially young men, to seek the company of and develop friendships with young women. Male friendships, although indisputably an integral part of one's life, can only go so far. Sure, I enjoyed the company of Ezequiel, Evaldo, and Enrique but that was not enough.

My friend Octaviano, who also shared my passion for motorcycles, lived a few short blocks from our house, so I often visited his family. His father was an electrical engineer and they had a very modern house. Since I visited his home with increased frequency, I soon developed a deep friendship with Vivian, his younger sister.

Vivian was special in many ways. Her complexion was as light and smooth as fine porcelain, her hair was auburn, and her eyes were the color of honey. Yes, she was a beautiful girl, but in my eyes what made her special were the circumstances in which she had been born. From the first day her parents realized that there was something wrong with her, and it was soon discovered that she suffered from congenital circulatory problems. Throughout her life she endured several operations, some performed in the Unites States, to correct that malady but even after those procedures she still walked with a limp.

These reverses did not get her down; she was always in a good mood and loved music and dancing. With time I came to confide in her all those concerns that teenage boys have. She would listen to me patiently and then offer a very sober and mature comment that went beyond her years. It was nice being able to share with Vivian all those confusing and often contradictory feelings that boys never share with each other, especially in a culture where men are not supposed to show emotion, but are always required to project an appearance of strength and invulnerability.

This tenuous, but real link continued even I after I left Cuba for the United States. During those first few months, when the shock of separation was still fresh, she would answer my letters and continued to offer emotional support, just as she had done in person. I also corresponded with Enrique on a regular basis but the tone and subject matter of those letters were quite different from those I exchanged with Vivian.

In 1963, relatively soon after my departure, I received a letter from my mother informing me that Vivian had died and how sorry she was. The particulars were rather sketchy. Apparently, she came home from school one day, told her family that she did not feel well, and went to her room. A doctor was called, but by the time he arrived, Vivian had died in her bed.

I was desolate. Just thinking about how young and vibrant she was, how much she loved life, made me question the fairness of the situation. Why would God choose to take her at such an early age? I still ask myself that question.

But this was not the last blow I would have to endure that year. A short time later, once again my mother wrote to give me more bad news. Enrique had died in a tragic accident. A jeep he was driving had overturned and he had been crushed. That is all she said; there were no more details about the accident.

My two best friends were gone; there was nothing I could do about it. I realized that after my departure, even though there was physical distance between us, communication still existed. Further, the hope of seeing them again in a not too distant future was still alive. With this news, even that hope had been snatched away from me. Once again, I was reminded of how precious, how ephemeral, and how unfair life is.

Even after all these years, I still keep their letters. The odd thing is, though, that whenever I read them I feel that somehow I am intruding, that they are addressed to someone else. Enrique and Vivian are not writing to me, to the man who writes these lines today; they are writing to that *other* young man who long ago, in a distant place, called himself their friend, and that time and circumstances shaped into someone they would probably no longer recognize.

SORPRESAS/SURPRISES

The year 1960 brought with it two very unexpected events but they had nothing to do with the political situation in Cuba. The path that the government was pursuing was very clear by then: the total suppression of any form of criticism, elimination of private property, and the creation of a machine that would ultimately control every aspect of daily life. To this end, the jailing and execution of potential dissenters had increased dramatically.

The *Instituto* was still open, so we continued attending classes and doing homework in spite of the deteriorating situation. Everyone kept hoping, although these opinions were never voiced out loud, for a radical change. The elections that had been promised at the beginning of the previous year never materialized.

Final exams were scheduled for the month of May, so it was a time when we spent many hours reviewing the material we had covered throughout the year. Given the rigorous and comprehensive nature of these exams, we formed study groups that met in different houses.

It was precisely at that time that Uncle Justo was admitted to the hospital in Havana. He had expressed a desire to see me—I was his godson—but I could not get away because of exams. Since his ailment was not supposed to be a serious one, I sent word that as soon as exams were over I would visit him.

That visit never materialized, for he died unexpectedly a few days later. I attended an all-night wake in Havana and the following day the casket with his body was brought to Pinar del Río, where the burial would take place.

It was a sunny day, and after a funeral mass at the San Rosendo Cathedral, the funeral cortege made its way to the cemetery. The cars parked outside the wrought iron gate and we made our way to the Albet mausoleum. On the way, we walked by the grave of the boy who had fallen off the roof while flying a kite, and I remembered all those times I had asked Tía Mercedes to let me stop to look at the colorful marbles embedded in the stone. That day, however, those memories seemed distant and faded.

By the time we arrived at the burial site, the cemetery workers had readied everything. After all the mourners had arrived, the casket was lowered into the ground and the heavy lid returned to its place. I still could not believe the Uncle Justo was gone; I kept thinking of how he had expressed a desire to see me but I had put off the visit because of final exams.

After the funeral and burial, we returned home; life would not stop, even before the inevitability of death. A somber mood pervaded everything. My mother, especially, was affected deeply since she and her older brother had always shared a special connection.

What happened three days later is an event that I question even to this day. Late one night—I had already been asleep for hours—I felt a hand squeezing my foot lightly. When I opened my eyes the first thing I saw was the chest of a man standing in front of my bed. Even half asleep I realized that it could not be my father; he never wore regular ties, but bow ties. As I raised my gaze, I saw Uncle Justo. I also knew that it was late, since my father's reading lamp cast some light on the hallway and now it was off.

I was petrified with fear (this cliché is quite accurate). Dead people do not come back; they are gone forever. Yet, there he was, standing in front of me, wearing the same dark suit and tie in which he had been buried. My heart started racing wildly; I closed my eyes and started reciting mentally every prayer that I had learned during my preparation for first communion, invoking divine protection during that moment of sheer terror.

When I opened my eyes again, hoping that he would not be there, he had not moved. The expression on his face, I noticed, showed no emotion. He just stood at the foot of my bed, looking at me, without saying a single word. Once again, I closed my eyes and repeated the prayers, but when I opened my eyes once more he was still present. I know that I should have tried to speak, to ask him what he wanted, but at that instant, faced with an experience that contradicted everything I had learned, I only thought of clutching the sheets and closing my eyes.

When I opened my eyes for the third time, he was gone. For days afterwards, I was afraid to go to sleep, thinking that the experience might be repeated. Eventually, somewhat reticent to talk about it, I confided in my mother. I thought she might think that I was making everything up, but her reaction upon hearing my recounting of the events was just as unexpected as Uncle Justo's visit.

She did not seem surprised at all but simply reminded me that he had asked to see me before his untimely death. She also emphasized the point that there was nothing to fear. I reminded her that once people die they disappear from this world; they become inaccessible to the living, no matter how much we miss them.

181

Without refuting my argument, she simply told me a story of a time when she was in her teens and still living at home with her parents. Through the open door of her bedroom, part of the living room was visible and she would often see, just before dawn, a young man sitting in one of the rocking chairs. He was no one she had seen before, and certainly he was not part of her family.

She inquired, and then described the person she had seen, down to his bad complexion. To her surprise, she was told that she was describing a former resident of the house who had died at a young age. Perhaps she was trying to convey to me the belief that there are certain things that go beyond logic but that nevertheless are as real as those activities in which we engage every day. From that day on I did not feel fear anymore, just curiosity. Somehow, I wanted and expected another visit but it never materialized.

The second unexpected event that year had nothing to do with Uncle Justo or events that defied all logic. That fall, my father had a heart attack. Fortunately, he survived and the doctors prescribed uninterrupted bed rest for six weeks. It was then that I realized that he was not invulnerable, that there were certain aspects of life that not even he could control.

Since he required constant care, someone had to be in the room with him at all times. We took turns caring for him, making sure he was comfortable and that the bedpans that he required were always available and clean. During those nights that I sat in the room while he slept, as I listened to his irregular breathing, I wondered how he had managed to endure the past two years and if he would survive this setback. My mother, of course, was always by his side and his friends, especially Luis Mendoza, stopped by the house on a daily basis to make sure we did not want for anything.

Eventually, after a long and slow process, he got out of bed and took his first feeble steps. Before long he managed to shave, take a regular bath, and put on one of his suits. I noticed that he had lost a lot of weight but that he was getting stronger by the day. Perhaps I had been wrong and my fears had been unfounded; again I started to believe that he was almost invulnerable and that he would always be there, no matter what.

RESISTENCIA/RESISTANCE

By then I had come to realize—in view of the deteriorating political situation—that something had to be done to oppose the policies of that cadre of thugs who had usurped power and were systematically undermining every democratic principle on which the Cuban nation had been founded.

But what?

Diagonally from our house, on the other side of Independence Park, lived a doctor—his first name was Rogelio—with his wife and two daughters. The girls were older than Luis and me, and from time to time I had visited their house because Margarita, the younger one, occasionally gave piano recitals in their living room. She had jet-black hair, a light complexion, and was always very soft spoken. I had heard her practicing for years, since due to the warm climate, windows and doors were usually open and our houses were relatively close.

One day, I struck a conversation with her and she openly expressed her dislike for the current regime; further, she said that we should do something about it. I now realize that the reason she was so open with me was because she was well aware—as was everyone else in town—of my father's difficulties with the people in power. We both knew that such talk could land you in jail indefinitely. Of course, I agreed with her but added that I had no idea how to proceed.

She then confided in me that she was already engaged in the resistance. I was not surprised, so I asked for further details. She was not shy about it and explained to me that she had a mimeograph machine that she used to print information exposing the unconstitutional policies of the current government. Further, she needed people to distribute these leaflets throughout the town. Was I interested?

Here was the opportunity that I was looking for, so I said yes. Once again, I knew that if these flyers were found either on my person or at my home, it meant immediate and unavoidable jail time. Understandably, I was scared; this was serious business and once I got involved, there would be no turning back. We agreed that I would return to her house the next day.

I kept all this to myself; experience had taught me that the fewer people involved, the better it was. In case I was found out, no one else would be implicated. Now that the commitment had been made, I had to figure out a way of distributing these subversive pamphlets without calling attention to myself. That aspect of the operation would be completely my responsibility.

By the time I picked up the flyers the next day, I had already figured out a way. I still marvel at how cool and composed Margarita was about the whole thing. She certainly had a lot more courage than I did, or maybe she was better at hiding her fear. She reminded me, although I already knew it, that it was best to get rid of the flyers as soon as possible.

Every day, on my way to and from the *Instituto,* I had to traverse the entire length of *Calle Real,* the main street of the town. On either side of the street there were always parked cars, and even though they were locked, their window glass was lowered a few inches to allow the relentless heat of the Cuban sun to escape. I took advantage of these partially open car windows to surreptitiously drop the pamphlets, which I had previously folded, inside the vehicles. I never stopped, but did it with a fluid motion as I walked by. The best place to hide was in broad daylight.

Another favorite place to carry out this clandestine distribution was the Riesgo Theater. Every Sunday, beginning at one o'clock, they held matinees that lasted until six in the evening. During those occasions, several movies were shown and many people came in and out of the theater. Some stayed for the entire show while others came at different times, depending upon the film they wanted to see.

During those matinees, I would visit the restroom several times, trying to use as many stalls as possible. There, I could leave with impunity the flyers that I carried inside my pants or tucked in my socks. I had no idea if what I was doing would change anything, but at least I was doing something.

Subversive activities, no matter how well planned and executed, cannot go on indefinitely. There is always a pattern that eventually will be discovered and traced back to the perpetrator. This is precisely what happened in my case. Fortunately for me, when this happened I had already left for the United States.

In a letter my mother wrote that two men from the secret service had come to the house asking to see me. This was always bad news, but as polite as she was, she informed them that I was not home at the time, but if they wanted, they were welcome to sit down and wait for my return.

ISIDRO

B y the beginning of 1961, the general situation had deteriorated further. A few months before, the Cuban government had nationalized all foreign properties, and as a result, diplomatic relations between Cuba and the United States had ceased. Many household products that before had been easily accessible—deodorant, soap, razor blades, etc.—had disappeared overnight from the store shelves. Most of the sugar produced in Cuba had been purchased by the U.S. at above world-market prices, so this sudden turn of events, now that its main customer had been eliminated, placed a tremendous strain on the Cuban economy.

There was also a rumor going around that the current government intended to take away the *patria potestad*, or parental rights, so they could do whatever they wanted to with the children. Given their current track record, this possibility was not a difficult one to believe.

It was around that time that the decision was made that Luis, Ezequiel, and I should leave the country and go to *El Norte*, a term that most Cubans used when referring to the United States. The process was not a simple one. Besides getting a passport, the right vaccinations, and an exit permit, the plane ticket had to be purchased in advance. Cuban currency could not be used—only American dollars were acceptable. Once all these requirements had been fulfilled, one had to wait for the official telegram containing the date of the flight. No one knew if the government had a system for assigning these dates since they appeared to be completely random.

The best thing to do, however, was to have a suitcase ready just in case.

I continued going to classes at the *Instituto* during the day, doing homework, and visiting friends. I also started studying English more seriously since the undeniable reality of my impending trip could not be ignored. My father had given me a self-teaching method called *Inglés Básico* and I made it a point to devote time to it every afternoon. The book used a phonetic approach and it also provided the student with a core group of verbs in the English language. Every lesson contained a self-test, and by the end of the program, I had acquired a rudimentary knowledge of the language. These hours spent on that course would prove invaluable later since they would provide a foundation for my studies and make the transition from Spanish to English less traumatic.

It was no secret among my friends that I had already secured my passport and that I had applied for the necessary exit papers. This was not unusual; by then many of our acquaintances had already left, including Evaldo.

Early one evening, while at a café that I frequently visited, I ran into some friends from the *Instituto*. We struck up a casual conversation and they told me that they were on their way to visit a *bayú*, which is what Cubans call a brothel. Of course, they invited me to come along, alleging that I could not possibly leave the country without visiting such an establishment.

I had no idea where such a place was located, and how much such a visit would cost me. They told me not to worry, that the place was not far. Further, if I needed money, they had me covered.

Once again that underlying belief that above all things I had to be a *macho* came into play, so I readily agreed to go with them. We left the café and went to the corner to wait for the bus that would take us part of the way. We did not wait long, and once we got on I realized that we were going in the direction of La Coloma, the coastal town where Luis Mendoza had taken us so many times for driving lessons a few years earlier. Eventually, the bus stopped in the parking lot of Tota's Bar. That was the end of the run; now it would go back to Pinar del Río and return an hour later.

My friends got off and I followed them, but I knew that this could not be the place. We did not go into Tota's Bar but started walking on the road towards La Coloma. About fifteen minutes later, faint under the moonlight, a very white house became visible. The path that led to the front door was covered by flat river stones that seemed to phosphoresce in the night. There was also the sound of distant music. On the way there we ran into other men traveling in the opposite direction, like nocturnal pilgrims who had already made their secret offerings at the foot of an ancient and forbidden altar.

The house proper lacked any sign that would identify the clandestine enterprise within. It was just a regular white house set back about fifty meters from the highway. I wondered how my friends knew of its existence.

The living room was no different from any other except that a jukebox had been placed against one of the back walls. Women in their underwear walked around, talking to the men who smoked or listened to the music.

Occasionally, a man would approach one of the women to ask

her if she was busy. Apparently, this was the predetermined signal that would lead to a more intimate exchange.

One of my friends, having selected a woman that he liked after a quick survey, approached her confidently and asked the same question. Within minutes they disappeared down a hallway that led to the rooms in the back of the house. My other friend did the same, and he also disappeared, accompanied by one of the women, into one of the rooms.

I was left alone, surrounded by people I did not know. For an instant I thought about just waiting for them and then going home without fulfilling the very purpose of my visit. I remembered my experience at Tota's Bar a couple of years earlier and my brother's forceful admonition: *¡No seas maricón!*—Don't be a faggot! A real man—a *macho*—would always rise to the occasion.

Propelled by this belief, which was reinforced by youthful exuberance and natural curiosity, I approached one of the women and asked her if she was busy. She said no—probably realizing that I was a first timer—and led me down the hall to her room. After closing the door, she asked me for the money. This was just a harsh reminder that what was about to take place was not motivated by feelings of any kind, but simply by an opportunity for profit. It was not love, but barter. Once I turned over the two pesos, she told me to take off my clothes and lie down on the bed.

I was extremely nervous, but as I had the opportunity to examine the room more closely, I was surprised almost to the point of being shocked. Sure, there was the double bed, nightstand and dresser with accompanying mirror. These were all common items, but what was most unusual was the small but elaborate altar—the effigy of the Virgin Mary had fresh flowers and votive candles at its base—that was mounted on one of the back walls. This was surely not a church or place of worship, but an out of the way brothel. The obvious incongruity reached the point of contradiction.

By then I was already on the bed and the anonymous woman was next to me, naked and stimulating me expertly. The exchange did not last long; the eagerness of youth, combined with my complete lack of experience, resulted in a total lack of control.

By the time I got dressed and returned to the living room my friends were already there waiting for me. We left the house and walked back to Tota's Bar where the bus would take us back to town. I can't recall if I made any comments about the experience, but I don't think I did. Somehow I felt that I had lost something precious, something irreplaceable, and that I had received nothing in exchange.

When I walked into my house, nothing had changed. Yet, everything was different; I was not the same young man who had left a few hours earlier. In the corner of the living room, still resting on its carved wood pedestal, was the bust of Isidro. It was then that I realized that he would never come back to life. I had lost my innocence and it was impossible for me to ever get it back, thus condemning him to remain a statue forever.

Many years later, in an attempt to make sense of that absurd experience, and searching for an answer as to why that young prostitute had an altar to the Virgin Mary in her room, I would write the stories *The Death of Isidro* and *Prayer*. These stories, as with all fiction, were pure conjecture on my part, so the questions still remain unanswered.

INVASIÓN/INVASION

O n the morning of April 15th, 1961, the residents of
Havana woke up to the sound of anti-aircraft gunfire
and bombs exploding. The news that the planes of the
Cuban air force had been targeted, and most of them destroyed,
soon spread throughout the island. Several B-26 bombers had
flown sorties from Central America to accomplish this task. The
Cuban air force—mostly made up of Soviet Mig 17s—did not get
a chance to get off the ground. This was but a preamble, everyone
knew, to the invading forces that would soon land. Now that
the Cuban planes had been destroyed, their task would be a lot
easier.

The Cuban regime, which by this time had declared itself
communist, was quick to react. Fearing an internal uprising, it
swiftly rounded up anyone suspected of not being a sympathizer
and placed them under arrest. No probable cause, no evidence
of guilt, but just mere suspicion often based on hearsay. Those
dissenters who escaped the nation-wide dragnet were forced to
go underground indefinitely.

Local jails and prisons, without a doubt, did not have the
capacity to hold so many detainees, so theaters, warehouses,
baseball stadiums, and any other large enclosures were used to
accomplish this purpose. The threat of an internal revolt, if not
completely nullified, had been greatly diminished.

My father, of course, was one of those who had been identified as someone who did not look upon the regime favorably. We feared that at any time the police would show up and carry him off to jail. After all, they had done it before and these were extreme circumstances, so the current government would have no compunctions in doing whatever was expedient to ensure its survival.

Surprisingly, that did not happen. They dispatched two soldiers to our house, to be stationed there twenty-four hours a day. Without saying so, and without providing any explanations, they were in fact placing my father under house arrest and constant scrutiny. Everyone who came to the house had to identify himself and provide a reason for his visit. So much for democracy and personal rights. To this day I still marvel at how much they feared what he might do; I also realize that at this point in his life, my father was a seventy-four-year-old man recovering from an almost fatal heart attack and no matter how much he wanted to, he could not control the destiny of the Cuban nation. All he could do was sit, wait, and hope.

On April 16th the invading forces—all made up of Cuban exiles—landed on Playa Girón, a swampy spot on the southern coast of Cuba. From there they started to make their way inland. Their steady progress was largely due to the air cover being provided by American planes, which flew to and from a nearby aircraft carrier located in international waters. It was just a matter of time—or so everyone thought—that the regime, facing the advancing forces and internal opposition, would implode.

Then, the unthinkable happened. The air support provided by the Unites States, a key component to the success of the operation, was abruptly and inexplicably withdrawn, leaving the invading forces defenseless. Retreat was not an option since they were trapped between the enemy and the ocean. To this day, there is a general speculation as to what happened and an underlying resentment in the exiled Cuban community given president Kennedy's decision to recall the planes that were providing the air cover, thus leaving the troops on the ground completely without support.

Within seventy-two hours the invading forces were surrounded and captured. Afterwards, there were endless speeches as to how Cuba had defeated the imperialist forces of the Colossus of the North, footage of Playa Girón, where the conflict had take place, and live coverage of the captured men, in shackles, being led into prison.

As a reprisal and warning to the general population, lest they consider an uprising, the executions were intensified and many of those who had been jailed remained there without formal charges or due process.

Things had definitely taken a turn for the worse.

ADIÓS/GOODBYE

The summer of 1961, without a doubt, was the most pivotal in my life. In the middle of July I finally received a succinct telegram informing me that at the end of the month I would be leaving Cuba. This decision, as I mentioned before, had not been solely my own, since I had just turned seventeen. My parents, after much consideration and anguish, had come to the conclusion that there was little future in a country whose government had openly embraced communism.

All Cubans, after the failed U.S.-sponsored Bay of Pigs invasion that previous spring, were feeling the repercussions. Many of those who did not sympathize with the regime had been quickly imprisoned without due process; others had had to go underground in order to survive. On the other hand, the supporters of the new system had become more entrenched in their views and less tolerant of dissenters.

After all these years I can't remember anything specific about the day the telegram arrived; in all probability it was a day like any other. My suitcase had been packed for months since the assignment of departure dates did not seem to follow any logical pattern. According to the telegram, I was scheduled to leave on July 26.

Around the 20th of the month, before dawn, I left the town of Pinar del Río to spend my last days in Cuba with my aunt Nena in Havana. My parents did not come with me since they had to stay with Luis and Ezequiel.

What I remember most vividly about my aunt's house was the deep silence, almost as if the entire structure had been somehow completely isolated from the outside world. By this time Tía Nena no longer lived in the old section of Havana, but had moved to a single-family house after marrying a Spaniard by the name of Barreiro.

Now I realize that being the oldest of eight siblings and never having had any children of her own, she had had a lifetime of practice holding back her words and going about her business without disturbing her surroundings. The only audible sound was the subdued murmur of her voice coming from her bedroom as she said the rosary in the afternoons.

I had almost a week until my flight. Since I did not know the city or have any money, the thought of going out never occurred to me. My aunt would not have allowed it anyway; I had become her responsibility during those last few days on the island.

The first few nights I had trouble getting to sleep, but I attributed it to the fact that I was in a different bed and in a different house. Perhaps it was just my subconscious mind fully aware that something momentous in my life was about to happen.

To pass the time during the day, I tried watching the old black and white TV set that was kept in the living room but soon grew tired of the propaganda that was being constantly broadcast on every channel. It was then that I found an old record player that my aunt kept in the dining room. As far as I can remember, the only record available was Tchaikovsky's *Nutcracker Suite*. When I first discovered the record player, I had hoped to find with it an assortment of popular Cuban music, so I was understandably disappointed at the more than limited selection.

I sat down and placed the needle on the first grooves. At once the soft, delicate opening bars filled the room. From the very beginning the ineffable quality of the music spoke to me, allowing me to remove myself momentarily from my situation and escape to a remote place where I was beyond the reach of anyone and anything. I was grateful to that 19th century Russian for having composed such beautiful piece of music.

From that day on, I found solace in *The Nutcracker Suite*. Although I loved the entire composition, my favorite piece by far was *The Waltz of the Flowers*. Without words, the music seemed to mirror perfectly the way I felt at that moment in time, when my entire future was an uncertain path filled with question marks every step of the way.

As the day of my departure approached, the news that Yuri Gagarin, the Russian cosmonaut was coming to Cuba was all over the news media. Because of his visit, all flights to the United States were being postponed by two days. I would not be leaving until the 28th. Once again, circumstances beyond my control had changed my plans. I did not watch the parades and official ceremonies on television, nor listen on the radio to the speeches full of empty rhetoric and grandiose promises. Once again, I sat in the semi darkness of my aunt's dining room listening to *The Nutcracker Suite*.

From that time onward, I would always associate that piece of music with that last week I spent in Cuba. Invariably, it would always evoke feelings of sadness and nostalgia whenever I heard it. That perception would not change until forty years later, after seeing my daughter Marisa dance the role of Clara during a Christmas presentation of *The Nutcracker*. From then on, that music would arise very different feelings, but all of them associated with a joyous occasion. At that time, obviously, the furthest thing from my mind was an unborn daughter who would come into my life so many years later.

When the day of my departure finally arrived, my parents miraculously appeared. They had made the three-hour journey from Pinar del Río to see me off.

At the airport, all passengers were placed in a waiting room with glass walls. There was no turning back now. On the other side, I could see my parents holding hands. They were more painfully aware than I was of all the unknown hardships that I would have to endure. Yet, they were certain that the decision to leave was the right one.

With me was my cousin Cecilia, Tía Estrella's younger daughter, who was only nine years old at the time. After stepping into that glass enclosure, she had become my responsibility. I remember her as a skinny kid who clutched her favorite doll, maybe not fully aware of what was taking place; she too was about to be separated from the rest of her family.

A soldier, noticing the doll, asked Cecilia if he could look at it, but as soon as she handed it over, he forcefully yanked its head off. I suppose he was looking for contraband, but there was nothing there. Cecilia, now faced with a decapitated doll, was about to start crying, but I quickly replaced the head and handed the doll back to her. God forbid that a nine-year-old child should endanger the Glorious Revolution!

A short while later, two soldiers came into the waiting room and called my name. As I stood up they signaled me to follow them. In an adjacent room, my suitcase lay open on a bare table. Plainly visible were the extra shirts, pants and shoes that I had packed earlier, as well as the book *Inglés Básico* that my father had given me.

"Is this yours?" asked one of them in an official tone. He was holding a shaving kit—another gift from my father when I turned fifteen.

I answered affirmatively, not knowing what was so special about that item. "In the name of the Glorious Revolution," he intoned lowering the pitch of his voice, "we are hereby confiscating these razor blades. You can get some more in that imperialistic country where you are going."

After that brief but meaningful incident I realized even more that I had made the right decision.

Before boarding the plane, the passengers were required to empty their pockets. Anything deemed of value would have to be left behind. In my case, the obvious item was the gold watch that my mother had given me when I entered the *Instituto*. I was compelled to remove it and place it in a wicker basket, joining the valuables that had been stripped from other passengers. Next, I had to show the contents of my wallet. This had been a present from Tía Panchita; she had bought it during one her trips to Mexico. The wallet was beautifully embossed with the Mexican sunstone and other national motifs. I feared that I would have to leave that too, but after removing all the money they returned it to me. I guess that The Glorious Revolution had no use for an empty wallet.

Eventually, we boarded the plane. I remember telling myself, "Take a good look; you might never see Cuba again." As I looked back I saw my parents, still holding hands behind the glass plate.

I would never see them again.

The plane took off right on schedule. As the buildings became smaller, I saw the tops of the royal palms, softly swaying in the warm breeze. In my mind, they were swaying to the music of *The Waltz of the Flowers*.

Then the island itself disappeared, occluded from view by a thick bank of clouds.

At that moment, as I caught a last glimpse of Cuba fading in the clouds, and conscious that I had abandoned everything and everyone I ever loved, I realized that all I had left were the limitless possibilities of a future that had yet to unfold.

REFLEXIONES/REFLECTIONS

S ome say that Cuba was a paradise, a view I will neither affirm nor deny. If I were to agree with such a statement, I would also be agreeing to a role of a modern-day Adam who was cast out of an ideal existence at the age of seventeen for a sin he did not commit. Should I adopt the opposite position, then my role would be that of a naïve young man who abandoned his country rather than opposing more forcefully the changes that were taking place after 1959. Maybe the truth lies somewhere in between.

I believe that for us Cuba is no longer just a geographical place, but rather a state of mind that was born from physical distance, the passage of time, and the inevitable distortion of memories. All of us Cubans who left the island, whether we like it or not, share that state of mind, an undeniable perspective of reality we cannot shake, no matter how long we stay in our adoptive country, how completely we embrace its customs, or how well we speak its language.

Kierkegaard was right. The passing years have provided me with those pieces that turned into my life. I have made all the connections, scrutinized every detail. They have coalesced into an inescapable portrait that openly shows, for all to see, accomplishments and failures.

Everything is clear.

Yet, I occasionally wonder about that potential other who could have been had I not boarded the plane so many years ago. Most certainly his life would have been very different from mine. Part of that naïve teenager is always with me, the old man who writes these lines today in a strange language, sharing this duality that circumstances imposed upon us. But we go on—there is no alternative—silently drawing strength from the memories of those left behind and from the love of those who surround us.

Inside of my Cuban passport

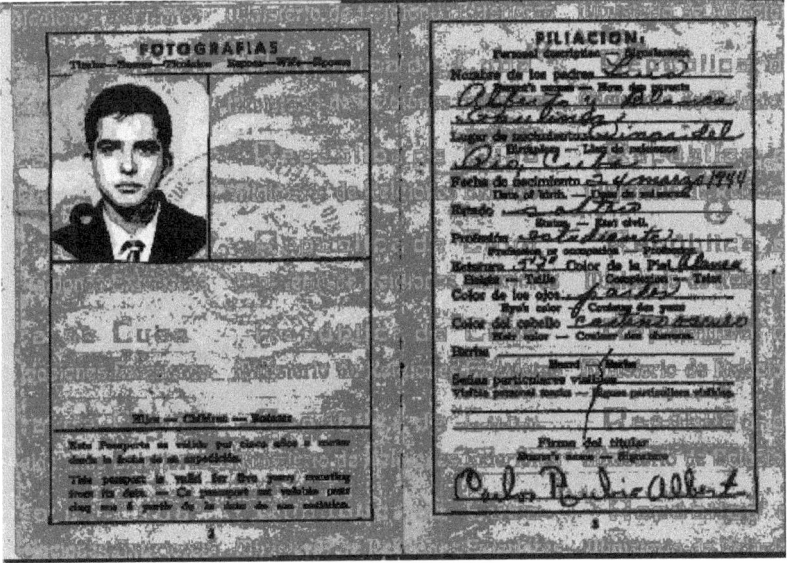

My parents, Blanca and Luis Alberto

Luis in his Boy Scout Uniform

Vivian and Enrique, my closest friends

About the Author

Carlos Rubio was born in Cuba and came to the United States in 1961. After finishing high school, he attended Concord College and West Virginia University. A bilingual novelist, in Spanish he has written Caleidoscopio, Saga, Orisha and Hubris. In 1989 his novel Quadrivium received the Nuevo León International Prize for Novels. In English he is the the autor of Orpheus's Blues, Secret Memories and American Triptych, a trilogy of satirical novels. In 2004 his novel Dead Time received Foreword's Magazine Book of the Year Award. In 2014 his novel Forgotten Objects was published by Editions Dedicaces. Since then he has completed two Spanish-language novels, Only the Voice and Double Edge.